Has Steven's phony map led to real treasure?

"I have something important to tell you," Elizabeth told Steven. "It's about your map. The treasure map you found at the park. Remember how you couldn't find it the next day, and you thought you'd lost it?"

Steven nodded. "Sure."

"You didn't lose it," Elizabeth said with a serious expression. "Jessica stole it."

Steven bit back a grin. So his plan was working! "No," he gasped.

"Yes, it's true. And what's more, she's already very, very close to finding the treasure. I saw her at the beach this afternoon. She found the first clue—a rock with a note attached to it. And she was about to find the second when I left," Elizabeth said in a whisper. "After she does that—well, she's practically found the pot of gold. And that's your pot of gold, Steven. You'd better check it out before it's too late!"

Steven widened his eyes. What did she mean, Jessica found the first clue? The map was a fake. Wasn't it?

SWEET VALLEY TWINS

Jessica's Lucky Millions

Written by
Jamie Suzanne

Created by
FRANCINE PASCAL

BANTAM BOOKS
NEW YORK · TORONTO · LONDON · SYDNEY · AUCKLAND

To Benjamin Markowitz, Johnny's friend

RL 4, 008-012

JESSICA'S LUCKY MILLIONS
A Bantam Book / March 1997

*Sweet Valley High® and Sweet Valley Twins® are
registered trademarks of Francine Pascal.*

Conceived by Francine Pascal.

*Produced by Daniel Weiss Associates, Inc.
33 West 17th Street
New York, NY 10011.*

Cover art by Bruce Emmett.

ISBN: 0-553-48436-2

Published simultaneously in the United States and Canada

*Bantam Books are published by Bantam Books, a division of Bantam
Doubleday Dell Publishing Group, Inc. Its trademark, consisting of the
words "Bantam Books" and the portrayal of a rooster, is Registered in the
U.S. Patent and Trademark Office and in other countries. Marca
Registrada. Bantam Books, 1540 Broadway, New York, New York 10036.*

PRINTED IN THE UNITED STATES OF AMERICA

OPM   0 9 8 7 6 5 4 3 2 1

One

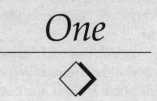

Jessica Wakefield tossed a pair of dice into the air and watched as they rattled onto her desk.

"Seven," she said out loud. She felt a surge of excitement. In the Sunday night movie she'd just watched, tourists visiting Las Vegas had struck it rich by rolling sevens and elevens. Maybe she could do the same thing. OK, so she couldn't afford to make the trip to Las Vegas, and she was probably too young to gamble. But there had to be some way she could make her luck work for her.

What about the lottery drawing that was held every night on the news—the one she'd just seen? Couldn't she win that, if she tried really, really hard? That way, she wouldn't even have to leave Sweet Valley.

She jumped out of her desk chair and went

down the hall to her twin sister's room. "Elizabeth," she said, walking in without bothering to knock. "Help me!"

Elizabeth was lying on her bed, and she looked up from the book she was reading. "Help you what? Learn how to knock before barging into someone's room?"

"Elizabeth, we're beyond knocking," Jessica said, straddling the desk chair. What was the point of having an identical twin if she couldn't tell when you were coming down the hall to see her?

Not that she and Elizabeth were all that similar—even though they looked identical, with shoulder-length, shiny blond hair, blue-green eyes, and matching dimples. Jessica was the risk taker of the two—she'd much rather be figuring out a scheme to become rich than lying on her bed, reading her social studies textbook. She spent most of her free time shopping and gossiping with her friends in the Unicorn Club, a group of girls who considered themselves the prettiest and most popular in Sweet Valley Middle School.

Elizabeth liked hanging out with her close friends too, but sometimes she liked reading books and writing for their school's newspaper just as much. But despite all their differences, the twins still considered themselves best friends.

"So are you going to help me? Please?" Jessica demanded.

"With what?" Elizabeth asked.

"What do you know about odds?" Jessica said, fiddling with a pen on Elizabeth's desk.

Elizabeth shrugged, dropping her book onto the floor and sitting up on her bed. "Not much. Why?"

"Well, I just saw this movie about winning big at casinos," Jessica explained. "And then right after that, there was the lottery drawing on TV, and all of a sudden, I thought—"

"That you should be doing your homework instead?" Elizabeth asked.

Jessica frowned at her. "*No.*" Sometimes Jessica thought that Elizabeth studied so much, she might as well be in college. "What I thought was, here are all these people, being lucky and making all this money . . . and here I am, totally broke. I mean, why can't I have some of what they have?"

"Well . . . " Elizabeth looked dumbfounded.

"So what I'm wondering is, could you help me pick out some numbers for my lottery ticket?" Jessica asked. "I figure I could roll these dice over and over and see which numbers come up most often. Then I'll know what the odds are, and I'll win the lottery! Right?"

Elizabeth looked at Jessica skeptically. "I don't know, Jess. I think the odds are going to be against you," she said. "Haven't you ever read the fine print on those TV ads? They're about four million to one—no, worse than that. You'll never win."

Jessica frowned. "Well, you don't know that. Somebody has to win, right? So it could be me.

Anyway, can't you just be supportive for once and help me figure out the math? Here, we'll start rolling the dice, and we'll write down the combinations that come up the most—"

"But Jessica," Elizabeth interrupted. "You're not eighteen years old. You have to be eighteen to buy a lottery ticket."

Jessica threw up her hands. "Minor detail! I can get someone else to buy the ticket. Like Mom, or—"

Elizabeth laughed. "Oh, yeah. I'm sure Mom would love to support you in your gambling habit."

"It's not a habit, OK?" Jessica shook the dice and rolled them onto Elizabeth's desk. "If I can get the odds figured out, I'll only have to buy a ticket *once*." She rolled the dice a few more times. "So far it seems like nine comes up a lot."

"What about the fact that the dice only go up through twelve, then?" Elizabeth asked. "Isn't that a problem?"

"Why?" Jessica replied.

"Because the lottery numbers go up a lot higher than that," Elizabeth pointed out. "Like, into the thirties and forties, I think. So how will you figure those out?"

Jessica frowned at her sister again. "I don't know! That's why I came in here in the first place. I thought you could help me."

"OK, here's an idea," Elizabeth said.

Jessica sat up straighter. Finally, Elizabeth was getting the point! "What?" she asked.

"Maybe you could write down the page numbers of our social studies textbook," Elizabeth said, picking up her book from the floor. "You know, the section we're supposed to be reading tonight about Irish history and legends?"

Jessica rolled her eyes. "As if that would work." Who could think about social studies when she had a lottery to win?

"Fine, don't help me," she told Elizabeth. "But when I strike it rich, don't come to me asking for a loan."

"Oh, I won't," Elizabeth said with a smile. "I'll come to you asking you to pay me back for all the loans I've given you!" She started giggling.

Jessica stood up and marched out of the room. "Very funny," she muttered. *When I become a millionaire, I'll have the last laugh. Not to mention a mansion with dozens of closets, eighty pairs of shoes, and the biggest pool in the neighborhood.*

And I won't let Elizabeth swim in it!

As soon as Jessica left her room, Elizabeth closed her textbook and put it back on the floor. She liked reading about Irish legends, but she was more interested in reading something else.

Elizabeth had discovered a story by an Irish writer named Maggie Sullivan called "Fool's Paradise." The tale came from a collection of stories Elizabeth's aunt Helen had given her for her last birthday. Elizabeth was planning to make a play out of it, for extra credit in social studies class. It was the saddest, most romantic story she had ever read.

Elizabeth grabbed the book from her nightstand. She'd already read the story three times, and each time she loved it even more.

In the story, which is set nearly a hundred years ago, a teenaged boy and girl want more than anything to leave Ireland and move to America. They finally achieve their goal, stowing away on an ocean liner. But once the ship lands in the United States, they become separated in a crowd and never see each other again. The story ends with the girl standing on the corner of a busy street, looking at every face that passes, realizing she's lost everything in coming to America.

What Elizabeth liked best about the story was the vivid, lyrical writing. She got such a sense of history, and a feeling for life in Ireland. It was teaching her more than any textbook ever could.

Elizabeth read the story again. Then she closed her eyes, picturing the world that the main characters must have lived in, what they looked like, how they spoke. . . . She felt as if she were right there.

No doubt about it—Maggie Sullivan was one of the best writers she'd ever read.

"Now, if I just shine this light over there . . ." Steven Wakefield adjusted his desk lamp so that it was pointing right at him as he stood in front of the full-length mirror. Perfect. He wanted to be in the spotlight.

Steven turned to the left, curling his arms, clenching his fists as tightly as he could. Was he mistaken, or were his biceps getting stronger by the hour? He turned to the right, checking out his profile. Not bad, considering he'd only started his special strength-building exercises a week ago. In another few weeks, he was going to be a flat-out stud!

Steven crouched lower, flexing his muscles the way the guys in weight-lifting contests did. He stared at his reflection in the mirror. No one else in the ninth grade at Sweet Valley High was going to be as strong as he was. He raised his fists in the air, swiveling from left to right. "Oh, yeah," he said, nodding at his reflection.

All of a sudden, Steven heard a strange sound— as if someone were choking!

He turned around and saw his little sister Jessica standing behind him, right in the middle of his room. She was holding her hand over her mouth, while her body quaked with laughter.

When she saw Steven looking at her, Jessica started laughing even harder. She curled her arms in the air, and turned from side to side. "Ooh, look at me, I'm Mr. Muscleman!" she said in a bad German accent. "I am very puny, but when I grow up I want to be big and strong!"

Steven glared at her. He could feel his face getting hot, and when he glanced at it in the mirror, he saw it was turning beet red. "Have you ever heard of knocking?" he demanded. "Or is that too advanced a concept for your *puny* mind?"

"Maybe my *mind* is puny, but at least *I'm* not," Jessica said. She giggled. "What do you think you're doing, training for the Olympics or something? As *if,* Steven! The only Olympics you're going to get into are the Wimp Olympics. The O-Wimp-ics!" Jessica doubled over, she was laughing so hard.

"Ha ha." Steven folded his arms across his chest. "Well, don't sign yourself up for any Brain Bowls just yet, Miss Mindless."

Jessica finally managed to stop laughing. She looked at Steven, wiping a tear out of the corner of her eye.

"So, what was so important that you had to come in here and interrupt me, without even knocking first?" Steven demanded.

Jessica held out her hand. "These."

Steven opened his fist, and Jessica deposited a pair of dice in his hand. "What's so important about a pair of dice?" Steven asked.

"I'm going to get rich, using those dice," Jessica told him. "And I want you to help me."

"Uh . . . yeah, right, Jessica. I'm sure," Steven said. "What are you going to do, make earrings out of them? Start a whole new fashion craze?"

"Hey, not bad." Jessica patted him on the arm. "So you have been reading those magazines I leave lying around."

"As if I'd waste my time—," Steven began.

"I'm talking about luck, Steven. I want you to help me figure out how to win the lottery," Jessica continued, interrupting him. "See, if I keep rolling the dice—"

"You want me to roll these?" Steven held up the dice. "You want me to help you, after you just barged your way in here, spying on me, making fun of me—"

"Hey, I didn't mean anything by it," Jessica protested. "So what do you say? Will you help me roll the dice?"

Steven juggled the dice in his palm. "OK, sure. I'll roll them. Just let me . . . find the right surface . . ." He walked over to his desk. Then he lifted up his hands and shook the dice up and down, so they rattled against each other loudly.

Jessica was looking at him eagerly, as if she couldn't wait another second to see what the roll would be.

Steven brought his arms back down so that he'd be able to throw the dice more accurately. "Are you ready? Here goes!" He turned, flinging the dice straight out the window and onto the front yard below.

"Steven!" Jessica cried. "Those are my lucky dice!"

"So go get them!" Steven said. "And stop bugging me!" He followed Jessica to his bedroom door and slammed it shut behind her. Then he turned the small lock on the back of the knob.

Some people don't know how to respect privacy. Some people think they can just go around mocking people in their very own bedrooms.

Jessica is going to pay for this . . . big time.

Steven peered out the window at Jessica, who was on her hands and knees, searching for her dice in the dark. This was only the beginning!

Two

Jessica jumped up from the couch at the sound of the doorbell. She rushed over to the front door and opened it wide. Outside, the sun was shining and the birds were chirping—but who cared about that? There was a man standing on her lawn, carrying balloons and a giant stack of hundred-dollar bills!

"Excuse me, are you Jessica Wakefield?" he asked in a deep voice. On top of everything else, he was cute too!

"Yes, I'm Jessica," she said, smiling at him.

"Congratulations, Jessica! You've just won the World's Biggest Sweepstakes! Here's five hundred thousand dollars!" he said, handing the stack of money to Jessica. "And by the way, would you like to go to a movie with me tonight?"

Jessica smiled, chewing on the end of her pencil. *Hey, if you're going to daydream, you might as well daydream* big.

Unfortunately, it was Monday morning, and she wasn't winning the sweepstakes. She was sitting in social studies class. Mr. Nydick was lecturing about Irish traditions, and all Jessica could think about was establishing a winning tradition of her own—and fast.

Isn't there a computer program to figure out the lottery odds? she wondered. If they could write programs to play solitaire and other card games, couldn't they compute how to win the lottery?

Jessica tried to think of the smartest person in her class, the person who did the best in math. If only she could pay that person to figure out which numbers to choose. Jessica could cut her or him in for a percentage of the winnings, maybe ten percent, then—

"Excuse me, Jessica, but what exactly are you working on right now?"

Jessica jumped in her seat. Mr. Nydick was standing right next to her, his hand on her right shoulder.

She scrambled to cover her notebook with her hand. "Oh, uh, nothing," she said quickly.

"Nothing? That's funny. I could have sworn you had a bunch of numbers written down," Mr. Nydick said, peering at Jessica's desk.

"N-Numbers?" Jessica sputtered. "Oh, well,

yeah. See, I was working on . . . my math home-work!" How could a teacher get mad if you were doing homework? Even if it wasn't for his class, it should still count for something.

"Hmm. Somehow that didn't exactly look like something Ms. Wyler would assign," Mr. Nydick mused. "But even if it were, Jessica, you're in social studies class right now, and that's what you should be focusing on."

Jessica nodded. "Yes, Mr. Nydick."

"Have you heard anything I've been saying about Irish legends?" Mr. Nydick asked.

Jessica cast a hopeless glance across the class-room at her twin. "Uh . . . that they're legendary?"

The classroom sounded with muffled laughter.

Mr. Nydick cleared his throat. "Yes. Well. That's certainly true. However . . ." He scratched his chin for a minute. "To help you focus, perhaps you could write a page-long essay about the legend we've been discussing today. In case you don't re-member, it's the legend about a pot of gold. One page, on my desk, tomorrow. *Single* spaced."

Jessica stifled a groan. A whole page on boring Irish history? Who wanted to write about a pot of gold anyway? Jessica was too busy trying to find one!

"You're writing a play?" Amy Sutton asked Elizabeth as they sat down for lunch in the cafete-ria on Monday. Amy was one of Elizabeth's best friends. "A whole, entire play?"

"Well, I don't know if I'll get that far, but I can definitely write a few scenes," Elizabeth told her, taking a bite of an apple.

"What's it about?" Amy asked, unwrapping her cheese sandwich.

"It's based on this story called 'Fool's Paradise,'" Elizabeth started to explain.

"'Fool's Paradise,' huh? Wait—don't tell me," Amy said. "It's about the Unicorn Club going to the mall. And they find this big sale, and it seems like paradise at first. Only the clothes turn out to be really ugly!"

Elizabeth laughed. She glanced over at the Unicorns' table, where Jessica and her friends were sitting in a small cluster. Neither she nor Amy liked many of the girls in the Unicorn Club, which they privately called the Snob Squad.

"OK, I'm sorry for interrupting. What is your play about?" Amy asked.

Elizabeth took a sip from her carton of apple-cranberry juice. "Remember that Irish writer I told you about? Maggie Sullivan?" Amy nodded. "I'm writing a play based on her story, for extra credit. The story's about two people who live in Ireland and want to come to the States—"

"Excuse me," Amy said. "Did you just say extra credit?"

Elizabeth nodded. "Yeah. You know how Mr. Nydick said we could do something—"

"Like you need any extra credit," Amy teased. "You

have a 99.999 average. *I'm* the one who needs extra credit. I've gotten B minuses on my last three papers."

"OK. Well, you could star in my play, after I write it," Elizabeth suggested.

Amy shook her head. "I can't act."

Elizabeth smiled. "Dress up like a leprechaun?"

"No way!" Amy said.

Elizabeth shrugged. "How about finding a four-leaf clover?"

Amy laughed. "Hey, if I could be that lucky, I wouldn't need extra credit, would I?"

Jessica was walking down the hallway after her last class Monday afternoon when she saw Rick Hunter standing in front of his locker. Rick had blond hair and blue eyes. In Jessica's opinion, he was one of the cutest guys in the entire school.

Of course, Jessica and Aaron Dallas were sort of going out, but she didn't see why she should be tied down to one guy when someone as cute as Rick was around.

She paused at Rick's locker and smiled at him. "Hi, Rick. What's up?"

"Oh, hi, Jessica." Rick tossed a few books into his locker. "How are you doing?"

"Good," Jessica said. *Better, now that I'm talking to you!* she thought, gazing at Rick. He looked so adorable in his baggy blue jeans, black-and-gray striped T-shirt, and black suede skateboard sneakers. "How about you?"

"I'm cool," Rick said.

No kidding, Jessica thought. *That's exactly what I was thinking!*

"Hey, there's a basketball game tonight at Sweet Valley High," Rick continued, casually closing his locker. "Some of the guys and I are going. Maybe you and Lila would want to go too. Should be a lot of fun."

Jessica smiled. Was Rick actually asking her out? Sort of? Kind of? "That sounds great," she said. "I love basketball." *Especially when I get to watch it with you!*

"The game starts at seven," Rick said. "Maybe we could meet at Casey's first, or something. You know, go over there together. What time would be good?"

"Oh, anytime," Jessica said with a wave of her hand. "I've got the whole night free!"

Behind her, she felt a tap on the shoulder. She turned around and saw Mr. Nydick standing there. "You've got the whole night free, as soon as you finish your essay," he said with a friendly smile.

"Essay?" Jessica repeated feebly.

"The one on Irish legends," Mr. Nydick reminded her. "Two hundred and fifty words, and no less. On my desk tomorrow morning, before class." He smiled at Rick and Jessica. "Well, have a good night!" Then he marched off down the hall.

Jessica collapsed against the row of lockers. How was she supposed to have a good night when she was slaving over an essay? Of all the luck. Just when Rick was asking her out!

"Drag," Rick commented. "I guess you can't make the game now."

"Drag doesn't begin to describe it," Jessica said with a sigh. "A whole essay in one night?"

"Is it for extra credit or something?" Rick asked.

"Kind of," Jessica said with an uneasy smile.

"Well, don't sweat it. There's another game next week," Rick said.

"Sure," Jessica said. "Of course." But would Rick invite her to the next game too?

I hate social studies! she thought, watching Rick walk away. *It's ruining my social life!*

Three

◇

"But Da, I have to go."

"Siobhan, you can't leave. Mother and I need you. What are you going to do so far from home?"

"I'll be all right. I'll remember everything you taught me."

SIOBHAN WIPES A TEAR FROM HER EYE

Elizabeth tapped her pen against the notebook. *Did that sound authentic?* she wondered. Or did it sound like she didn't know what she was doing? Turning Maggie Sullivan's story into a play was a lot harder than she'd thought it would be. She had to make up a lot of the dialogue herself, since the story had more description and detail than dialogue.

She felt like a fool, trying to imitate her idol, Maggie Sullivan. As if she could be good enough!

Elizabeth quickly skimmed the few pages she'd written. Well, maybe it wasn't that bad. Maybe all she needed was to hear it spoken out loud, read like a scene should be. Then she could decide what to leave in and what to take out.

She got up from her desk and headed straight for Jessica's room. "Jessica?" She knocked on the door. "Can you help me?"

"I'm busy," Jessica replied, opening the door with a frown. Loud music was blasting out of her radio. "I'm working on my essay for Mr. Nydick."

"With the music that loud?" Elizabeth asked. "I thought you were dancing."

"Some of us study with music," Jessica said in a haughty voice. "Some of us don't need total silence."

"Well, excuuuuuuse me," Elizabeth said. "Hey, do you have a minute? I need you to run through my play with me. Here, if you could read the father part—"

"I'm working on my essay," Jessica said. "Sorry!" She slammed the door in Elizabeth's face.

Of all the nerve! Elizabeth thought. Jessica was constantly interrupting her to ask for help with homework. And the one time Elizabeth asked for help, Jessica was too busy? Talk about selfish!

Forget Jessica. What I really need is a male voice anyway, to play Siobhan's father. She walked down the hall to Steven's room.

Elizabeth paused outside his door. What was

that gasping noise? It sounded like somebody was having trouble breathing! She flung open the door. Steven was on the floor, doing one-arm push-ups. His face was bright pink, and his T-shirt was soaked in sweat. "Are you OK?" Elizabeth asked.

Steven looked up at her, straining to hold himself up with his right arm. "Huh?"

"You sounded like you were dying," Elizabeth said. "Are you OK?"

"Of course," Steven said, his arm shaking violently.

"Oh. Well, whatever you say." Elizabeth shrugged. "It's just—maybe you should take a break for a little while."

Steven collapsed, landing on the floor with a thud. "Well, uh, maybe I will take a break. Not that I need to or anything. Actually, I'm supposed to rest in between my strength-building exercises."

"Right," Elizabeth said with a smile.

Steven sat up and glared at Elizabeth. "What's that supposed to mean?"

"Nothing. I just thought maybe you could take a break and help me with my play," Elizabeth said. "Since you're supposed to rest and all." Steven looked like he'd pass out from exhaustion if he exercised one second longer.

"I am," Steven said. "It says so in my book." He pointed to a paperback on his bed called *Go for the Gold in You!*

Elizabeth thought Steven might be better off

going for the bronze, but she decided to hold her tongue. She did want Steven to do her a favor, after all. "OK, well, here's the thing. I'm writing a play." Elizabeth held up her notebook, showing Steven the pages she'd written so far. "I was wondering if you could help me do a reading of it, so I can see how it sounds."

"I'm busy," Steven said. "You already interrupted my regimen, just when I was getting up to my last ten push-ups—"

"Like you would have been able to do them!" Elizabeth said. "You were practically in the ambulance when I came along. You're lucky I interrupted you."

"Lucky? To be asked to be in your play?" Steven rolled his eyes. "Oh, yeah, I'm so lucky. I'm just thrilled. And I'd like to thank everyone in the Academy for this award and—"

"You know what? I'm glad you're busy. I'll find someone better to read my lines," Elizabeth said, her face burning up. "I'm sure you'd ruin the whole thing anyway! Go back to your push-ups, Steven. But if you're looking for the gold in you, you can forget it. You might as well start looking for the copper!"

Elizabeth turned on her heel and started to walk away.

"Elizabeth, wait!" Steven called.

She stopped, turning around.

Steven was standing in his doorway. "Please let

me be in your play, pretty please? It's always been my dream to be on off-off-off-off-off-off-off Broadway!" He cracked up laughing.

Elizabeth glared at him. Why had she ever expected that Steven would help her in the first place? "Well, if you keep up your *act* of pretending to be an athlete, maybe you'll get there someday!" she said.

Why did she have to get stuck with such unhelpful siblings anyway?

Jessica flipped through her textbook to the chapter Mr. Nydick had assigned. What a way to start off the week! Not only did she have to write an essay, she was missing valuable time with Rick. Teachers had no hearts.

There was nothing to do but concentrate, she decided. The sooner she got this out of the way, the sooner she could move on to other, more interesting things. Like sleeping.

According to the legend, whoever finds the pot of gold will be rich forever. But so far, the pot of gold hadn't been found. That doesn't mean it doesn't exist, the textbook went on to say. It suggested that perhaps the pot of gold stands for something else—that possibly the legend means that the search is more important than finding the gold.

"Since when?" Jessica mused. She'd been searching for her own private pot of gold ever since she was born.

The book went on to describe different versions of the legend that had been passed down through time. Jessica closed her eyes, envisioning the pot of gold. Wouldn't it be amazing if she found it someday? And why shouldn't she? Just because her ancestors came from Sweden, not Ireland . . . the book didn't say anything about having to be Irish. And it *was* almost Saint Patrick's Day, which had to mean something.

What if she started wearing lots of green clothes? She had a sweater that looked awfully good with her eyes . . . and an old green turtleneck she could take out of storage, if that would help. . . .

Jessica had a flash of insight. Maybe the pot of gold hadn't been found because the right person hadn't looked for it yet! Maybe she was the one who was meant to find it. Maybe Mr. Nydick's assigning her this extra paper wasn't an accident!

Jessica believed one hundred percent that some things were meant to happen for certain reasons. And as soon as she figured out where to begin, she'd start looking for the pot of gold. She didn't have any time to lose.

She focused on her textbook again, jotting down all the details of the legend. Not just for her paper—for future reference!

I wonder if Mom and Dad would pay for me to go to Ireland, she thought. *Or maybe the pot of gold isn't even in Ireland, and that's why no one's found it yet!*

Jessica sat back in her desk chair, admiring her

own brilliance for a second. With a little bit of detective work—and possibly some travel—that pot of gold was going to be hers.

Forget winning the lottery. Hunks of gold were much prettier.

Steven could barely lift his feet as he trudged down the hall toward the bathroom. He had to soak in a hot bath, the book said, or his muscles might become tight. *Might? Tight? How about sore, aching, and totally overstressed?* Steven thought. The book didn't mention that.

"Lila, you should have seen the look on Rick's face when I told him I couldn't go to the basketball game."

Steven stopped in the hall outside Jessica's door. She was blabbing away on the telephone, as usual, even though it was a school night and she was supposed to be writing some dumb essay, which she'd complained about during dinner for an entire fifteen minutes.

"He was totally devastated," Jessica went on to her best friend.

Steven picked up one foot and tried to keep going. It felt like lead.

He didn't mean to eavesdrop—not really. He was just having a hard time making it to the bathroom, that was all.

And if he happened to hear something especially silly that he could use to embarrass Jessica for the next few days or so, well, hey, what was he supposed to do? It wasn't his fault that she was talking so loudly.

She should have shut the door all the way if she wanted privacy.

Anyway, ever since she'd barged into his room the other night, he'd been looking for an opportunity to get her back. She didn't know anything about privacy—respecting others' or safeguarding her own.

"Well, what could I do? I mean, there was Mr. Nydick, telling me I had to write my essay, and there was Rick. But he said we could go to a game next week, so I guess it wasn't a total loss," Jessica continued. "Actually, that's kind of the best news of all, that I stayed home, because I've been reading about the legend. . . . No, I haven't lost my mind. . . . No, this isn't Elizabeth. Quit it!" Jessica laughed. "See, this legend's all about a pot of gold, right? And it says all kinds of stuff about how if you follow certain clues, plus your heart and a bunch of meaningful junk like that, you'll find the pot of gold, and you'll be rich forever."

Steven shook his head. Jessica actually believed everything she read?

"Well, I know *you're* already rich for life, but *I'm* not," Jessica declared, sounding a little irritated. "Anyway, the book says that a lot of people believe there's a treasure map that's like several hundred years old or whatever. And whoever's lucky enough to find the map can find the gold. So I fig-ure . . . hey, why shouldn't that be me? I'm lucky, right?" She paused for a second. "Well, sure, but there was that time I won the door prize when that new music store opened at the mall—and what about when I won the Johnny Buck concert tickets? OK, technically Elizabeth won them, and I stole them, but—"

Steven smiled, finally managing to limp his way down the hall. *Jessica actually thinks she's going to find some old Irish treasure map—and a pot of gold?*

Man. She's even sillier than I thought.

Four

Tuesday afternoon, Elizabeth sat at the kitchen table, eating popcorn as she leafed through a book she'd picked up at the library. It was a short biography of Maggie Sullivan, written several years ago. Elizabeth figured that the more she knew about her favorite author, the better.

"After she and her husband moved to southern California, Sullivan suffered one of the greatest tragedies of her life. Her husband, Patrick, who had been ill, passed away quite suddenly, leaving Sullivan to start a new life in a foreign country all by herself."

Elizabeth gasped. That was almost like the story "Fool's Paradise"!

"Their love had been one of the driving forces behind Sullivan's creativity, and with Patrick gone,

Sullivan wrote less and less, for a time even dropping out of public sight," the author continued.

Elizabeth felt tears come to her eyes. Maggie and Patrick Sullivan had been childhood sweethearts! Their love had lasted their whole lives. She must have been completely and utterly destroyed when he died.

"What are you so sad about?" Steven walked into the kitchen. He'd been outside, shooting baskets in the driveway, and now he was carrying a set of small barbells. He set them down on the counter with a loud clang.

"It's this writer I like," Elizabeth said, wiping her eyes. "She really had a hard life."

"Yeah?" Steven opened the refrigerator and took out a bottle of sports drink, sounding completely unconcerned. "What writer?"

"Maggie Sullivan. She's from Ireland," Elizabeth explained.

Steven shrugged. "Never heard of her. So I guess she can't be *that* great."

Elizabeth frowned at Steven, one eyebrow raised. "Just because you haven't heard of her doesn't mean she's not great. Considering the last book you read was *Digging Out the Gold Medal Inside You*—"

"It's called *Go for the Gold in You!*" Steven corrected her.

"Whatever," Elizabeth said with a wave of her hand.

"And it's a good book," Steven said.

"Oh, yeah. I bet. I'm sure it's really hard to make lists of exercises," Elizabeth said. "And calories burned and muscle-tone ratios."

"I don't see you exercising," Steven said. "So you're not in a position to argue about that." He lifted the barbells off the counter and started curling them.

"And I don't see you reading," Elizabeth countered, picking up her book. "So *you* don't know anything about *that*."

"Fine!" Steven said.

"Good!" Elizabeth replied, pushing back her chair. "But just so you know? Maggie Sullivan *is* a great writer."

"Sure," Steven said with a snicker. "And *I'm* Arnold Weissenhammer."

"In your dreams," Elizabeth said, walking past Steven with her head held high.

"Lila, listen to this!" Jessica said excitedly. "The pot of gold will be found in a beautiful spot, filled with sunshine, surrounded by the sea. The ocean waves will crash nearby," she read from her social studies textbook. "What does that *say* to you?"

Lila shrugged, dragging a potato chip through the bowl of ranch dip Jessica had prepared for them after school. "That it could be anywhere?"

"No!" Jessica cried, breaking a chip in half. "Doesn't it sound *familiar*? Sun, green grass, surrounded by the sea?"

"Sounds like Ireland, I guess," Lila said.

Jessica shook her head back and forth. Did she have to explain everything? "Lila, it doesn't *say* that it's an island, does it?"

"Well . . . no, not exactly," Lila muttered.

"And isn't Ireland an island?" Jessica argued.

"I guess," Lila said.

"So? The pot of gold's not in Ireland, don't you get it? It's somewhere else entirely," Jessica argued.

Lila ate another potato chip. Jessica watched her as she ate another, and another—

"Lila! Are you going to help me or not?" Jessica demanded, feeling frustrated. She grabbed the bowl of dip and pulled it away from her friend. "We'll never find the pot of gold at this rate."

"He*llo!*" Lila cried. "Do you actually think we have a shot at this? I mean, I don't know what book you were reading last night, but mine didn't say anything about the pot of gold being in America, much less our backyards!"

"Great idea! That's what I'm talking about—brainstorming!" Jessica leaped to her feet and pushed back her curtain, staring out at the backyard. All she saw was Steven, doing laps in the swimming pool, his arms flailing in a wild crawl stroke. Was he swimming . . . or drowning? Jessica let the curtain drop and turned to Lila. "OK, so not in our backyards. Not in Ireland. That leaves . . ."

"The rest of the entire world," Lila said with a sigh. "Not to mention the cosmos, the ocean—"

"It's not in the ocean," Jessica said. "We've already established that."

"We have?" Lila asked.

Jessica nodded. "Trust me. Now, where would *you* hide a pot of gold?"

"In my closet," Lila said. "In a fireproof safe. No, correct that—I'd keep it at the bank."

Jessica frowned. Robbing banks wasn't exactly part of the Irish legend. She looked at her bookshelves for anything else that might provide a clue. "You know what we need?" she asked Lila.

"Some sodas?" Lila said, brushing salt off her pants.

"No. Lila, I'm looking at the big picture here," Jessica said. "And what I see is you and me finding the pot of gold. You donate it to me, of course, since you already have all the money you could ever spend."

"Wrong!" Lila cried.

"Wrong what?" Jessica asked.

"I don't have all the money I want," Lila said. "Why do you think I'm here helping you in the first place?"

"Because you're my best friend?" Jessica guessed.

"No. Because my dad put a limit on my credit card," Lila said with a loud sigh. "If you can imagine the gall."

Jessica smiled faintly. What she couldn't imagine was having her own credit card!

"I want a new leather jacket, and it's only three hundred and fifty dollars, but he said no way, and I said yes way, and—well, to make a long story short, I've been cut off," Lila confessed, a tear at the corner of her eye.

"Wow. I had no idea," Jessica said, soothingly patting Lila's arm. She shoved the bowl of dip back toward her friend. "So that means you want to find the pot of gold as badly as I do?"

Lila nodded eagerly. "Once I've got it, I'm going to say, 'Keep your dumb cards, Daddy. It's on *me.*'"

"Oh, yeah. Me too," Jessica said. After she paid back all of her debts anyway. If she had any gold left over. "Hey, I have an idea! Why don't we call Rick and see if he could help us!"

Lila shook her head. "No way. I'm not sharing with anyone. Except you, of course."

"Of course," Jessica said. A picture flashed through her mind of her and Lila each tugging at the pot of gold, until the handle came off and they had no way to carry it. "OK, so the legend mentions a map. First thing we have to do is find the map."

"Right," Lila said confidently. "Just find the map. But, uh . . . Jessica? If it's a really old map, wouldn't it have disintegrated by now?"

Jessica frowned. She hadn't thought of that. "Maybe they wrote it on some really tough, thick paper, or tree bark or something."

"If it's Irish, maybe it's on a green piece of paper!" Lila suggested.

"Good point. Of course . . . maybe it's written in Irish too," Jessica said.

Jessica stared at her textbook. Great. The last thing she needed was to have to translate something from Irish to English! "Wait a second. It's a map, right?" she said to Lila. "And maps have lines and big *X*'s and stuff—not words!"

"True," Lila agreed. "So what do we do now?"

Jessica leaned back against her bed. "I have no idea. But maybe Rick—"

"Give up already!" Lila said. "We're not cutting Rick Hunter in on this."

"Hunter . . . Doesn't that sound Irish? And he does have those freckles on his nose—"

"One freckle," Lila said. "I don't think that makes him an expert on Irish treasure maps."

"Hmm," Jessica muttered. "Well, in that case, we'd better hit the library tomorrow and—"

"The library?" Lila asked, as if Jessica had suggested they shave their heads. "Why?"

"Because! We need to do some research on this stuff," Jessica said.

Lila wrinkled her nose. "You're not roping me in for some extra-credit project you have to do, are you?"

"Don't be ridiculous," Jessica said. "We'd never be assigned something this useful."

"Girls? How's the homework coming?" Mrs. Wakefield knocked lightly on the door, then poked her head inside the room.

"Oh—fine, Mom!" Jessica said. "We're . . . making some progress." *Not nearly enough, but some,* she thought. They'd ruled out Ireland anyway.

"Well, how would you like to keep working here for a while, Lila, and stay for dinner?" Mrs. Wakefield asked.

"Sure," Lila said eagerly. "I'd love to. Thanks."

"You're welcome." Mrs. Wakefield smiled.

"Mom? Can we have corned beef and cabbage?" Jessica asked.

"Corned beef? Cabbage?" Mrs. Wakefield looked at Jessica, then at Lila, then back at Jessica. "Well, no . . . not tonight. I already made burritos."

"But sometime soon? Like this week?" Jessica pressed.

"But . . . I thought you hated cabbage." Mrs. Wakefield sounded confused. "Don't you?"

"It's not to eat, really. It's for inspiration," Jessica said.

Mrs. Wakefield stared at Jessica. "Inspiration? You mean . . . for Saint Patrick's Day? I didn't know it was so important to you."

Jessica winked at Lila. "It is now!"

"So what were you girls so busy studying for this afternoon?" Mr. Wakefield asked that night at dinner, handing Jessica a piece of blueberry pie. "Is there a big test tomorrow or something?"

"I hope not," Elizabeth said with a laugh. "Because if there is, I don't know anything about it." She took a sip of milk.

"Neither do I," Jessica said. "No, it's nothing like that. It's way more interesting. It's—" Jessica stopped herself. Why was she telling everyone about her and Lila's plan? The less other people knew about the pot of gold, the better.

"What is it?" Steven asked, scooping up some vanilla ice cream.

"Never mind," Jessica said, digging into her pie. "You wouldn't be interested."

"Oh." Steven shrugged. "Well, all right. Actually, something pretty interesting happened at the park this afternoon—I almost forgot to tell you guys."

Jessica rolled her eyes. "What? Did you manage to bench-press a pigeon?" She and Lila started giggling.

Elizabeth smiled. "Come on, Jessica. Don't tease Steven. He's sensitive about being a wimp."

Steven's face reddened. "I'm *not* a wimp."

"No, you're not," Mr. Wakefield said. "In fact, if you keep up with those exercises, I'm not going to be able to keep up with you."

"That's the plan, Dad," Steven said, sounding proud. "Anyway, as I was saying . . ." He glanced at Jessica.

"Go ahead," she said. "No one's stopping you." She smiled politely.

"Yes, tell us what happened at the park," Mrs. Wakefield prompted, frowning at Jessica.

Oops, Jessica thought. She'd have to remember

not to tease Steven so much—at least not when her parents were around.

"OK, so my friends and I were playing basket-ball, as usual," Steven began. "And when we were done, we went to sit down—you know, on those benches by the fountain? And there was this old *book* lying there. Someone must have left it there," he explained, with a meaningful glance around the dining room table.

"Hmm . . . fascinating," Lila said, licking her spoon.

Jessica stared at Steven. That was supposed to be a story? All his exercising was going to his head . . . and destroying his brain cells!

"That's not the whole story," Steven said patiently. "It's what happened next that's interesting. We kind of moved the book—you know, so we could sit down? And this really ancient-looking piece of paper fell out onto the pavement. It almost went into the fountain, but I grabbed it at the last second. Anyway, it was all yellow, and it had a bunch of lines drawn over it, and this giant X. It's like an old treasure map or something, I guess." Steven shrugged.

Jessica sat bolt upright in her chair. *A treasure map? Did Steven actually say he'd found a treasure map?*

"Did it look real?" Mrs. Wakefield asked. "Or was it a new map that someone tried to make look old?"

"Oh, it's definitely old. It's almost crumbly,"

Steven said. "I think it belonged to some girl named Erin, way back, because that name's written on the top."

Jessica was slowly chewing, and she nearly bit her tongue in half. Erin! Jessica had read in her textbook that Erin stood for *Ireland*. And that meant . . .

"Hey, a treasure map," Lila said, her eyes shining with excitement. "What a coincidence! Jessica and I—"

Jessica put her foot over Lila's and pressed down hard, flattening Lila's shoe. "What Lila was about to say is that she and I were talking about going to that new jewelry store at the mall called Hidden Treasures," Jessica said. "Or Forgotten Treasure or something like that."

Lila opened her mouth but then quickly shut it.

"There's no store with that name at the mall," Elizabeth said.

"It's *brand-new*," Jessica insisted. "It might not even be *open* yet." She turned back to Steven, trying to look as indifferent as possible. "So, uh, Steven, are you sure it's a map? I mean, what else do you know about it? Was it in a certain kind of book? Is that what makes you think it's . . . you know, Erin's?"

Steven's eyebrows crinkled. "Why do you want to know?"

"Oh—just—you seemed kind of sure about it and all," Jessica said.

"Well, I am," Steven said. "The book it fell out of

was some kind of big encyclopedia. I can't remember what it was called. *The History of Europe* . . . or *The Traditions of England,* or—"

Jessica was perched on the edge of her chair. "*The Folklore of Ireland?*" she guessed.

"That's it!" Steven smacked his palm against the table. "How did you know?"

Jessica shrugged, smiling uneasily. "Lucky guess?"

"So, can we see the map?" Lila asked.

Jessica pressed on Lila's shoe again. "Not that we . . . need to," she hurriedly added.

"I could show it to you later, if you want, but it's about to fall apart," Steven said. "I kind of want to leave it where it is."

"Which is . . . ?" Elizabeth asked.

Jessica stared at her, lifting one eyebrow. Elizabeth wasn't clued in to this pot of gold thing too, was she? But that was impossible—even Elizabeth couldn't think that fast.

"I locked it up in my desk drawer," Steven said.

"You locked it up?" Mr. Wakefield asked, sounding surprised. "Why? Is it valuable?"

"Who knows, Dad? It might be," Steven said.

It might be? Jessica thought. More like it is!

"Actually, it probably has really high historical value," Mrs. Wakefield suggested. "Maybe you ought to give the Sweet Valley Historical Society a call tomorrow. They might want to take a look at it."

Steven nodded, polishing off his slice of pie. "Good

idea, Mom. Maybe they'll know where it's from."

Jessica stared at her mother, and then at Steven. The *historical* society? No way! She wasn't about to let a bunch of boring old nerds get their hands on that map—not until she checked it out first.

Of course, that would mean taking it out of Steven's desk, which was locked.

Minor detail, she thought. *Nothing that will stand in the way of Jessica Wakefield.*

Five

Elizabeth scrubbed the glass pie plate and then handed it to her mother to rinse. "Did I tell you I found out that Maggie Sullivan moved to California when she was older? Southern California, even."

"No kidding," Mrs. Wakefield said, running the plate under the hot water. "How did you learn about that?"

"I got a biography of her from the library and read it this afternoon," Elizabeth said. She couldn't stop thinking about Maggie's life and how she must have felt losing her husband so suddenly. She'd give anything if she could talk to Maggie in person. Maybe she could even get some ideas for her play or write an article about her for the school paper. "Mom, do you think there's any way I could find her?" she asked.

"Hmm." Mrs. Wakefield rubbed the pie plate dry with a dish towel. "You know, I'm pretty sure there's an organization of local writers in town. You could call there and see if they know anything. Or else just leave a message asking Maggie Sullivan to call you. That way, you wouldn't be intruding on her. If she wants to get in touch with you, she can."

"Great idea!" Elizabeth said, feeling excited. "I'll call them first thing tomorrow morning."

"Why bother?" Steven said, walking down the stairs into the kitchen.

Elizabeth turned around and stared at him. Steven was wearing shorts and a tank top and his running shoes. "What do you mean, 'Why bother?'" she asked.

"If this writer is as famous as you keep saying she is, why would she want to talk to you?" Steven scoffed. "She's probably too busy writing her next book or something."

"She might be busy. On the other hand, maybe she'd appreciate meeting a fan of her work," Mrs. Wakefield suggested. "Not all writers are solitary creatures, you know."

"Mom's right," Elizabeth said. "And when she hears about my play for our special section on Irish studies, maybe she'll want to help me."

Steven snorted. "Well, I wouldn't hold my breath," Steven said.

Elizabeth glowered at him. Why did Steven always

have to shoot down her ideas? Did he think that was part of the job description for being a big brother?

Steven leaned down, trying to touch his toes. "You guys are really getting obsessed with all this Irish stuff. What's the deal anyway?"

"Oh, *we're* getting obsessed?" Elizabeth pointed at Steven, who was doing more stretching exercises. "At least we don't exercise twenty-four hours a day and only talk about things like strength and endurance."

"Yeah, well, at least I don't believe in leprechauns," Steven replied.

"OK, you two, why don't you give each other a break?" Mrs. Wakefield said. "There's no point arguing over nothing."

Elizabeth turned back to the sink and started scrubbing a plate with extra force. She hated the way Steven made fun of her! Especially about something as important as her love of Maggie Sullivan's work.

Elizabeth didn't normally believe in vengeance. But as she washed the salad bowls, she couldn't help wondering how she could get back at her brother. Tie the laces on his running shoes together so that he'd trip and fall? Add an extra hundred pounds to his barbells when he wasn't looking? Tell everyone he worked out with the Abominable Ab-Developer?

Whatever it was, it would have to be good—and soon.

*   *   *

Jessica heard the front door close with a loud bang. *Finally!* She was starting to think that he'd never leave.

She tiptoed down the hall and slowly pushed open the door to Steven's bedroom. The coast was clear.

Well, as clear as Steven's room ever got. It was almost as messy as her own, with clothes piled up all over the place. Unfortunately, thanks to Steven's new exercise routine, most of the clothes were sweaty—and smelly!

Jessica pinched her nose closed as she tiptoed over to his desk. The shades were pulled down, so she could hardly see. But Jessica didn't want to turn on the light. What if Steven were jogging down their street? If he saw the light go on, he'd know something was up.

And it was important to keep Steven in the dark for as long as possible, Jessica decided, even if it meant *she* was crawling around in the dark too.

She stepped over a giant pile of dirty athletic socks and practically fell right up against Steven's desk. Steadying herself, she groped along the surface of his desk and felt a small piece of metal. She straightened up and slowly opened her palm. It was a key! A small key!

That figures, she thought. Steven was probably in the middle of hiding the key somewhere when he was struck by the sudden need to run a marathon. *Fine with me if he's going to turn into Mr. Mush-Brain,* she thought, fumbling for the lock in the desk's top drawer.

She slipped the key into the lock and turned it back and forth until she heard a click. "Yes!" she whispered.

She slid the drawer open quietly, wincing as it screeched a bit. *Just one more second,* she thought, *and I'll get the map and get out of here.* Jessica's heart was pounding. This was a little bit too suspenseful for her. She felt like the hero in a spy movie. *The name's Wakefield . . . Jessica Wakefield.*

She reached into the drawer and pulled out a crackling, aged piece of paper. Holding it up to the dim light coming in through the shade, she spotted several jagged lines and small *X*'s. At the top, *Erin* was printed in large black letters.

Jackpot! she thought.

"Well, not yet," she muttered under her breath, laughing quietly. "But soon!"

She closed the drawer, being careful to leave the key exactly where she'd found it. Hopefully, Steven wouldn't decide to follow through on his idea to bring the treasure map to the historical society. She needed some time to study the map and find the pot of gold.

And then, it was off to the races! No, not the races—the mall! Any mall in the entire world! Did they have malls in Paris? Jessica wondered as she made her way back toward the door, carefully avoiding a bunch of compact discs strewn across the floor.

"*Aiiee!*" she cried, her big toe running smack into one of Steven's metal barbells. "Ow! Ow! Ow!"

Jessica clapped her hand over her mouth, her foot throbbing in pain. She had to be quiet or she'd blow everything!

Elizabeth was walking up the stairs when she heard a scream.

Jessica! she thought, recognizing the voice instantly. *What's wrong?*

She ran the rest of the way upstairs, only to find Jessica limping out of Steven's bedroom. "Jessica? Are you all right? What were you doing in there?" she asked.

"Shh!" Jessica said. Still hopping on one foot, she took hold of Elizabeth's arm, pulling her into her room. Jessica closed the door behind her and leaned against it with a loud sigh. "Phew! That was close."

Elizabeth peered at the piece of paper in her sister's hand. "What was close? What were you doing in Steven's room? I thought he was out jogging."

"He is," Jessica said, hopping over to the window. She pushed the curtain aside and looked out. "And with any luck, he won't be back for hours."

"Why does that matter?" Elizabeth asked.

"Elizabeth, I have to ask you something very, very important," Jessica said, limping across her bedroom. She sat down in her chair and placed the sheet of paper on top of the desk.

"Sure," Elizabeth said. "What is it?" She stepped over to Jessica's side and stared at the piece of paper. "Wait a second. Is that the map Steven was talking about at dinner? Did you *take* it?"

"Hold on! I didn't get to ask my question yet," Jessica protested. "Can you keep a secret?"

"That depends," Elizabeth said, "on whether you stole that or not."

"I didn't steal it." Jessica cleared her throat. "I *borrowed* it. I'll give it back . . . after I use it."

Elizabeth felt like she had missed something. "Use it? For what?"

"First you have to promise you won't tell anyone else about this," Jessica said. "You won't tell Steven I have this, you won't tell Amy what I'm about to tell you, you won't write this in your journal—"

"Jessica! You make it sound like a spy mission or something," Elizabeth commented.

"Exactly. That's *exactly* what it is." Jessica nodded gravely. "And that's why I need your total cooperation."

"Or what? You're going to turn me in to the other side?" Elizabeth joked.

Jessica didn't laugh. "Do you swear to keep this a secret or not? Because if you don't, you have to leave right now."

Elizabeth had no idea what Jessica was up to, but she definitely wanted to find out. Anything this secretive had to be at least a little fun. "I promise I won't say anything to anyone," Elizabeth said. "Now give! What's up?"

A wide grin spread across Jessica's face. "This is *it*, Elizabeth. This is the answer to all my problems. I won't have to play the lottery, or go to Las Vegas. It's all right here on this sheet of paper!"

Elizabeth glanced at the tattered, marked-up paper. "What is?"

"This is the treasure map to find the pot of gold!" Jessica said. "See? It says Erin on it, which means Ireland, and it's—oh my gosh! Look at this!" She pointed to a small shamrock in the lower right-hand corner. "And this!"

Elizabeth leaned over the desk, focusing on a tiny emblem that looked sort of like a soup pot . . . and sort of like a coffee pot. "That?"

"It's the pot of gold!" Jessica squealed with excitement. "All I have to do is figure out where it is. Maybe if I read this fine print . . ." She stared at the map and read out loud, "When the dusk appears, do not fear, if the ocean is clear, the treasure is near!"

She stared up at Elizabeth, her eyes wide. "What do you think that means?"

Elizabeth shrugged. "That whoever made up this map is a bad poet?"

"No!" Jessica said, sounding exasperated. "It's a *clue*, not a poem, silly. And if I can just figure out where it is, then I can follow these two little X's and find the treasure . . . all before Steven even realizes what he found."

"But Jessica," Elizabeth said. "There's no such thing as buried treasure. I mean, that's just a legend. A myth. It's not real."

Jessica tapped the map with her index finger. "Doesn't this look real? I didn't make this up. Steven found it at the park, and it did fall out of a book about Ireland, so it makes sense. And wouldn't it be horrible if I didn't even *try* to find the treasure, and someone else found it instead? I think it's part of the legend that when you find a treasure map, you have to follow it—no matter who or what gets in your way."

Elizabeth didn't remember reading that part, but she let it pass. "So you want to look for this . . . pot of gold or whatever. But Jessica, Steven's the one who found the map. So shouldn't *he* go in search of the pot of gold?"

"He did find the map. But he was also stupid enough to lose it," Jessica said smugly. "And anyone who loses the map, loses the treasure. That's the way it goes in all the legends."

Elizabeth wondered where Jessica was getting her information. She was about to suggest Jessica put the map back when she heard the front door slam.

"I'm home!" Steven yelled up the stairs. "Man, what a great run! I must have gone ten miles—in record time, too! You know, I think I'll run the L.A. marathon next year!"

Elizabeth frowned. She was getting pretty tired of Steven's boasting.

Jessica grabbed her arm. "You won't tell him I took it, will you? Please? Come on, Elizabeth—you promised."

Elizabeth thought about what a jerk Steven had been earlier, making fun of her for wanting to meet Maggie Sullivan. The way he'd been acting lately, he deserved to lose any treasure Jessica might find . . . even if it only turned out to be a reward from the Sweet Valley Historical Society.

"I won't tell him," she promised.

Jessica grinned. "You won't regret this, Elizabeth. When I'm rich, I'll remember how you helped me."

"Oh, I'm sure," Elizabeth said. "And you'll probably give me—what, a dollar?"

"Don't be ridiculous," Jessica said. "I'm not going to carry anything smaller than a twenty."

Six

◇

"Hey, has anyone seen my map?" Steven asked, coming into the kitchen on Wednesday morning.

Elizabeth nearly choked on her glass of orange juice. Jessica had just been stuffing the treasure map into her backpack a few seconds earlier.

"No, I haven't," Jessica said calmly, slinging her backpack over her shoulder. "Why?"

"Because, I can't find it," Steven said with bewilderment. "I could have sworn I left it in my room last night."

"Not just in your room," Mrs. Wakefield corrected him. "You told us you'd locked it up in your desk drawer."

"Right! That is where I put it," Steven said. "Hold on a second. I'll go check again." He ran back up the stairs, taking them two at a time.

Elizabeth looked at Jessica and raised her eyebrows. It looked like Steven was going to discover the map theft after all. "What are you going to do?" she whispered, once her mother had turned on the faucet to rinse her coffee cup.

"I'm not worried," Jessica whispered back. "I have a plan."

"What did you say, Jessica?" Mrs. Wakefield asked, turning around from the sink. "You have something?"

"Oh—I—uh, I have a . . . quiz today," Jessica stammered. "In social studies."

"That's what you and Lila were studying yesterday, wasn't it? So it should be no problem," Mrs. Wakefield said. "You'll probably ace it."

"Oh, yeah." Jessica shrugged. "I'm not worried."

Elizabeth had to admire how relaxed Jessica looked. If *she* were about to be caught by Steven, she'd be sweating bullets.

Steven clomped back down the stairs and into the kitchen. "That map isn't in my desk drawer. I don't know what happened to it."

"Well, maybe you put it somewhere else," Jessica suggested. "You know, another drawer. Like your sock drawer or—"

"No." Steven shook his head. "I could have sworn I put it in that top desk drawer. Then I locked the lock and put the key on the desk. . . ." He tapped his chin, thinking. "It's just not there anymore. Isn't that weird?"

Jessica shrugged. "Maybe you put it under your mattress for safekeeping—you know, like people did with money in the old days. Or maybe it's buried under some barbells or something." She looked at Elizabeth and winked.

And maybe it ended up in Jessica's room instead! Elizabeth thought. But she decided to go along with her twin. After all, ganging up on Steven was kind of fun.

"Jessica's right," Elizabeth said. "I mean, the map could be anywhere."

"But I swore I left it right in that desk," Steven said, still sounding puzzled.

"I'm sure it'll turn up," Mrs. Wakefield said. "Maybe you put it . . . in your closet accidentally. Or in a notebook."

Don't be so sure, Mom! Elizabeth thought. "Steven, I don't want to insult you or anything, but you are kind of forgetful," she said. "This wouldn't be the first time you thought you left something one place and it turned up another. Like the time you put your camera on the back of a bookshelf in the den—and you reported it stolen to the police?"

Jessica looked at Elizabeth and nodded her approval. "True!"

Steven frowned. "Well, yeah, but that was a long time ago."

"OK. Then what about when you forgot what you were cooking, and you put the eggs in the toaster and the toast in the frying pan?" Jessica asked.

"I was tired," Steven said. "It was six o'clock in the morning!"

"That's nothing," Mrs. Wakefield joined in. "When Steven was six, he forgot how to find his way home from school!"

Go, Mom! Elizabeth thought.

"That was a *really* long time ago," Steven said. "But I guess you guys have made your point. I probably did put the map somewhere else. I'll just have to figure out where. But it's a shame—I wanted to bring it by the historical society after school." He paused for a second. "Gee, I hope I didn't do something dumb, like throw it out."

"That would be terrible!" Mrs. Wakefield said, sounding genuinely concerned.

"Oh, yeah. Terrible. Just awful, really," Elizabeth added. "Imagine the loss to the historical society."

"It'd be a *tragedy*," Jessica said. "Maybe you should go upstairs and look through your trash can right away!"

"Nah. I've got to get to school. Anyway, you know what they say." Steven shrugged his shoulders. "Easy come, easy go!"

Elizabeth stared at him. Since when did Steven give up on anything so easily? Usually he was livid when his stuff was missing. He'd follow her and Jessica around for hours on end, accusing them of stealing everything he owned.

"Steven, are you feeling all right?" she asked. "Do you think maybe all that exercise is . . . changing you?"

"Sure it is." Steven curled his arms and struck a bodybuilder's pose. "I'm getting a *lot* stronger."

And a lot more mellow too! Elizabeth thought. "Well, OK. Whatever you say. I'll catch up with you guys. I want to call that writers' group first and leave a message for Maggie Sullivan," she said.

"Do you really think she'll call you back?" Jessica asked, sounding doubtful.

Elizabeth shrugged, picking up the phone book. "I don't know, but it's worth a shot. If she lives in California, I want to meet her."

"So. Where do you think this is?" Jessica asked Lila during lunch on Wednesday. She'd spread out the treasure map on a small corner of the table.

"I have no idea," Lila said, peering at the map. "It kind of looks like it might be near water."

"Well, duh," Jessica said. "It only says in the clue that when the ocean is clear, the treasure is near!" Really, if having Lila help was going to boil down to Jessica explaining every single thing to her, what was the point? She might as well have been working on her own. That way, she'd get to keep whatever she found.

"Sorry," Lila said, tossing her hair over her shoulder. "But some of us haven't been up all night staring at this thing. Some of us just saw it for the first time!"

Jessica drummed her fingernails against the table. She hated when Lila made good points. "OK, well you're looking at it now. So tell me what you see!"

Lila leaned over the map. "This kind of looks like a big tree, doesn't it?"

"So?" Jessica asked.

"So, I'm just telling you, there's a big tree . . . and it's near the ocean . . . and then there's something about dusk falling . . . ," Lila mused. "That's all we know."

Jessica stared at the map. That wasn't nearly enough information. "Hey, wait a second. What's that?" She pointed to some faint writing that showed through from the other side. Why hadn't she noticed that the night before?

Lila flipped the map over and read, "The treasure will be found by the person who follows the X's in order. Warning! If the proper order is not followed, the pot of gold will disappear!" She turned to Jessica, curling a strand of her long brown hair around her ear. "Disappear? What does that mean?"

"It means we have to figure this out, and fast," Jessica said, flipping the map back over to study it. How was she supposed to know which X to follow first? "One X is bigger than the other," she said. "So that means . . ."

"It's either first or second," Lila said. "Which leads us exactly nowhere."

"Don't be so negative! Think," Jessica commanded her. *A big tree on the coast at dusk*, she repeated in her head. But nothing was coming to her. She felt like her brain was buried in sand.

Sand, she thought. Maybe the treasure was buried in sand. Maybe it was at the beach! Dusk . . . a big tree . . . sand . . . Jessica must have seen a hundred scenes like that. Dusk . . . a big tree . . . sand . . .

Then suddenly one picture came into focus. Jessica saw a very large tree, perched on a rock, hanging out over the ocean. She saw a beach. She saw the sun setting. . . .

"Lila!" she cried, leaping out of her chair. "I know where it is!"

Lila grabbed her arm, pulling her back into her seat. "Don't tell the entire sixth grade, OK?"

Jessica could barely sit still, she was so excited. "Lila, you're not going to believe this."

"Probably not," Lila said, concern etched on her face. "But tell me anyway."

Jessica cupped her hands around her mouth and leaned close to Lila's ear. "It's Sunset Beach!" she whispered.

"It's what?" Lila said.

"Sunset Beach," Jessica said again. "All the clues add up. Dusk equals sunset. Ocean equals beach. It's like a word problem in math!"

"You hate those," Lila remarked.

"Not this time! Not when it's going to make us permanently rich!" Jessica said.

"OK. Tell me again why you think it's right here in town," Lila said, "when it could be anywhere in the world."

"Look, it makes total sense!" Jessica insisted.

"The treasure map was *found* here because whoever lost it was close to finding the buried pot of gold!"

"Wow. You think?" Lila asked.

"Definitely," Jessica said. "Somebody left the map in their book about Ireland. They were probably on their way to Sunset Beach when they lost their book. They'll never find the pot of gold without this map, and the X's—"

"What if they made a photocopy of the map first?" Lila asked. "They could be at Sunset Beach right now!"

Jessica's heart sank. She couldn't let someone else get to the pot of gold first!

Seven

"How's your play going?" Amy asked, sliding into a seat across from Elizabeth in the cafeteria.

"I kind of got stuck at one point," Elizabeth said. "I'm hoping I can talk to Maggie Sullivan about it. Maybe she can help me out of my writer's block. I called this writers' association and left a message asking them to call me with information, like her phone number. Maybe they'll get back to me— maybe they won't. I've got my fingers crossed."

"Hey, maybe Maggie Sullivan will even want to be *in* your play," Amy suggested. "You know, how sometimes directors get little bit parts in movies?"

"I don't know about that." Elizabeth glanced across the cafeteria. She could see Jessica and Lila hunched over the treasure map, studying it intensely. "Actually, something pretty interesting has been going on at my house in the past couple of days. Maybe that's why I haven't finished my play."

"What do you mean?" Amy asked, looking over her shoulder as she followed Elizabeth's gaze. "Is it Jessica?"

"You're not going to believe this," Elizabeth said. She felt a twinge of guilt. She *had* promised Jessica she would keep the map a secret. But Jessica was constantly promising to keep secrets for her and spilling them instead. Just last week she had told their father about a birthday present Elizabeth was planning to make him. And the week before that, Jessica had told Todd Wilkins that Elizabeth had a secret crush on him . . . and before that . . . well, it was too much to keep track of.

"Steven said last night at dinner that he found this ancient treasure map," Elizabeth began. "And Jessica's been reading all about the pot of gold legend. So she thinks the map Steven found is going to lead her to the pot of gold!"

"No way." Amy giggled. "No one's that gullible."

"She and Lila are studying it right now," Elizabeth said. "They're not even sitting in the Unicorner, so you know it's serious."

"That *is* serious," Amy remarked. The Unicorner was the table where the members of the Unicorn Club always ate their lunch. "They must really want to keep the map a secret."

Elizabeth nodded. "Jessica's planning on following the map and getting rich. I guess she doesn't want too many of her friends to share in the wealth."

"So . . . what does this map look like?" Amy wanted to know. "Does it look even halfway real?"

"Sort of," Elizabeth admitted. "It seems old anyway."

"And they'd really be upset if someone else took a look at it," Amy mused. "It would really get under their skin. Wouldn't it?"

A smile spread across Elizabeth's face. "What are you suggesting?"

"Hi," Elizabeth said, sitting down next to Jessica a few minutes later. "Mind if we eat lunch with you guys?"

"Well . . . uh . . . ," Jessica began, looking nervously at Amy. "Kind of." She raised an eyebrow at Elizabeth. "We're talking about . . . that thing. You know."

"Oh, sure. But I can tell Amy anything, and she won't tell a soul. Right, Amy?" Elizabeth asked.

"I have *no* idea what you guys are talking about," Amy said. "If that helps."

"It doesn't," Lila said snidely. "You shouldn't even be here."

"Well, uh, I do go to school here," Amy said, "so it's kind of hard not to be."

Lila frowned at her. "You *know* what I meant."

"So, can I look at the map?" Elizabeth asked. "Did you guys figure out anything yet?"

"Actually," Jessica said quickly. "We're—"

"Baffled," Lila interrupted. "Completely and utterly baffled. We have no idea what this thing means."

"Oh. Well, maybe I could help," Elizabeth said, peering at the map.

"No, thanks!" Lila said. "This is our problem, and we'll solve it somehow. I'm sure you're really busy—"

"Not right this second, I'm not," Elizabeth said. She was getting a kick out of making Lila so nervous. "Come on, I want to show Amy the treasure map. We're only going to look at it for a second. We're not going to memorize it or anything."

"You'd *better* not," Jessica said.

"Yeah. That's *our* gold," Lila insisted, finally taking her elbows off the map.

Talk about greedy! Elizabeth thought. The gold didn't even belong to them!

Amy leaned forward, staring at the map. "You think this leads to a pot of gold, huh?"

"Yes," Lila said, folding her arms across her chest. "And it's all ours."

"Oh, yeah, of course," Amy said. "On the other hand, if we figure out the map first—"

"Don't even think about it," Jessica said in a threatening tone.

"Chill out, you guys," Elizabeth said. "We don't want the dumb gold!" She studied the map. There was something familiar about it. The pen it had been drawn with had seeped through the thin paper—like a fountain pen.

Wait a second, she thought. *Didn't I just lend my blue fountain pen to Steven a couple of days ago?* And he hadn't given it back yet either.

One day Jessica was looking for treasure . . . and the next day Steven found a treasure map? Was that a coincidence? Or had Steven decided to make Jessica her very own treasure map?

"Well?" Jessica asked. "Do you have any ideas?"

"Actually, I do," Elizabeth said.

Both Lila and Jessica sat forward in their chairs. "You do?"

"Sure," Elizabeth said. "I think that Steven forged this map. I don't think it leads to anything."

Jessica glared at her. "You're just saying that to keep us from looking. Then you're going to run off after school and find the gold for yourself."

"No, I'm not," Elizabeth said. "I really think Steven made this up. See the color of the ink—"

"Blue? Oh, yeah. That's really unusual. I'm sure Steven's the only person in the world who uses *blue* ink," Lila said in a snotty tone. "Come on, Elizabeth, admit it. You're trying to throw us off the track."

Elizabeth sighed, frustrated. "Fine, you don't have to believe me. But don't you think it's kind of odd that you were looking for a map one day, and Steven found one the next day?"

"I never told him I was looking for a map!" Jessica said. "This is a complete coincidence. No—it's better than that. It's *fate*. And *you're* not standing in the way of fate." She grabbed the map out of Elizabeth's hands, like a two-year-old fighting for a toy.

"Jessica, you're acting like a real jerk," Elizabeth commented, staring in disbelief at her twin. "Is finding money the only thing you can think about?"

"Right now, yes," Jessica said. "I deserve it!"

"Why, because you stole a map from someone?" Elizabeth scoffed.

"A cheesy, phony-looking map?" Amy added.

"It's not phony, it's real," Lila insisted. "If it were phony, would it lead to a real place like Sunset Beach?"

"Sunset Beach, huh?" Amy asked. "Sounds like a good place to find a pot of gold. Or a bottle of sunblock anyway."

"See? They wormed something out of us already!" Lila complained. "Cheaters!"

"Anyway, what do you guys know about treasures? Nothing!" Jessica said. "I've been studying this stuff. Plus, I have a ton of things I'm going to buy when I find the gold."

"All for yourself, no doubt," Elizabeth muttered. She'd never heard her sister be so selfish in her entire life! Imagine if it *were* real gold! She would spend it all on herself, without thinking of anyone else.

"At least *we'll* know what to do with it when we get it," Lila said snobbishly. "At least *we* won't buy ugly clothes that are all blue, or books by old Irish writers, or other totally useless things!"

Elizabeth felt her face turn red. Her favorite color was blue! She was wearing a blue-and-white striped shirt and blue jeans!

She waited for Jessica to jump in and tell Lila she was over the top. She'd never let Lila talk to Elizabeth like that before. But Jessica didn't say a word in Elizabeth's defense.

"Jessica! Aren't you going to say anything?" she prompted her twin.

"Yes. Yes, I am," Jessica said with a self-satisfied smile. She folded the map into a neat square. "I have something very important to say to both of you, in fact. And that is . . . Get lost!"

Elizabeth stared at her twin. Here she'd been helping Jessica by keeping a secret from Steven, and this was what she got in return? Instead of being grateful, Jessica was acting completely self-centered.

She turned to her friend. "Come on, Amy, let's go," she said. "If we stand here any longer we might catch the greedy disease."

Jessica stuffed the map back into her backpack. Showing it to Elizabeth had been bad enough. She didn't plan on letting it out of her hands for the rest of the day. She wasn't about to lose the one thing that was the key to her happiness.

OK, maybe not her happiness, but close. Being

able to buy whatever she wanted, whenever she wanted, would make her pretty happy, wouldn't it? *Imagine Elizabeth calling the map a fake. She's just jealous.*

When she looked back up, Jessica saw her definition of happiness heading right across the cafeteria toward her—Rick Hunter! Jessica quickly shook her head to fluff up her hair. She hoped she was having a good hair day. She'd been too busy deciphering the map between classes to check the bathroom mirror.

"Hi, Rick!" she said.

"Hey, Jessica. Hi, Lila," Rick replied, stopping at their table. "Listen, since you couldn't make the game the other night, I was wondering if you guys wanted to go to Casey's after school."

"Sure!" Jessica said, thrilled. "That sounds great." Casey's ice cream parlor was one of Jessica's favorite places to hang out at the mall. Going there with Rick would be awesome.

All of a sudden, Jessica felt pressure on her foot. She glanced down and saw Lila doing the same thing that Jessica had done to her the night before—smashing her shoe on top of Jessica's! Only Lila was wearing her Dr. Martens, and it really hurt!

Jessica struggled to move her foot, but she couldn't budge it. "Lila?" she said through gritted teeth, still trying to keep the smile on her face for Rick. "You want to go to Casey's, don't you?"

"We can't," Lila said. "Not this afternoon. We have to do that—that *thing*."

"Well, we can put that *thing* off until tomorrow," Jessica said.

"What thing?" Rick asked, looking confused.

"It's nothing," Jessica said. "Just something we have to take care of, but it's no rush."

"But you said—," Lila began.

Jessica wrestled her foot out from underneath Lila's and stomped on Lila's shoe. "One more day isn't going to matter. So, Rick, we'll meet you at Casey's?"

"Yeah. Sounds good. How about at four?" Rick asked. "Peter and Ken are coming too."

"Cool," Jessica said, nodding. "See you at four!" She gazed at Rick as he walked back to his table. He had so many friends. He was really popular. And Jessica could see why. . . .

Once he was gone, Lila yanked her feet out from beneath the table. "You're giving me bunions. You realize that, don't you?"

"Bunions are on the bottom of your feet," Jessica observed lazily, still watching Rick.

"Then ingrown toenails," Lila said, rubbing her foot. "Which are totally going to make it impossible for me to wear my new sandals, so don't ever do that again."

"You're the one who started it," Jessica said.

Lila sighed heavily. "Listen, that isn't the point. The point is, we're supposed to go to Sunset Beach after school and dig for the gold, remember? What if someone has a copy of the map and gets there first?"

Jessica thought about it for a minute. "If someone else has a copy . . . they're probably at Sunset Beach right now. So it's too late for us anyway," she reasoned. "Or else they came here from Ireland, and they have no idea which beach to check out, and they're driving up and down the whole coast of California, looking for a big tree. I'm not worried."

"What about the fact that you just showed Elizabeth and Amy the map? If we don't get to Sunset Beach this afternoon, they will," Lila said.

"I don't think so," Jessica said. "I think we scared them off. Anyway, Elizabeth's too busy trying to meet some Irish writer to think about buried treasure."

"But—what if some kids are playing—and they start digging sand castles—and they accidentally find—," Lila sputtered.

"Lila, get a grip!" Jessica interrupted her. "The treasure's been buried for hundreds of years. It's not going to pop up in the next couple of hours. Anyway, we'll go there right after school tomorrow. It'll be waiting for us. I promise."

"Well . . . OK," Lila grumbled. "But if your date with Rick ends up costing us the pot of gold . . ."

"Don't worry so much. We'll get the gold," Jessica assured her. *And I'll get Rick.*

Eight

◇

Wednesday after school, Elizabeth threw open the front door and ran into her house. She had heard the telephone ringing as she walked up the sidewalk.

She grabbed the receiver of the phone in the kitchen. "Hello?" she said breathlessly.

"Hello?" an older woman's voice replied. "Is this Elizabeth Wakefield?"

"Yes! Yes, it is!" Elizabeth said. Was it her imagination, or did the woman have a slight Irish accent?

"Oh, good," the woman said.

"Are you from the writers' group?" Elizabeth asked eagerly. "Do you have information about Maggie Sullivan for me?"

"You might say that." The woman laughed a little, her voice cackling. "I *am* Maggie Sullivan."

"What?" Elizabeth gasped. She grabbed the kitchen counter to steady herself. She felt like she might faint.

"Yes, it's me," Maggie Sullivan said. "The writers' association passed on your message, and I'd be delighted to help you with whatever it is you're looking for. So tell me, what do you need?"

"Mrs. Sullivan, this is such a thrill," Elizabeth said. "I'm just trying to catch my breath!"

"Ah, no, dear. You mustn't call me Mrs. Sullivan. You must call me Maggie," she replied.

"M-Maggie, then," Elizabeth said. She quickly tried to remember the list of questions she'd written to ask the author, but she was too stunned to think of even one. "I've been working on a play," she began. "I mean—I'm writing one, based on your story 'Fool's Paradise,' which I love. I love all of your books, actually."

"Oh, you're too kind, my darling," Maggie said, cackling again.

Elizabeth noticed that her accent was half Irish, half American. Her voice sounded a bit strained, but Elizabeth decided that must be because she was nearly seventy years old.

"So what did you want to know, then?" Maggie asked.

"Um . . . uh . . ." Elizabeth felt a little nervous, talking to such a great writer. She took a deep breath, trying to compose herself. "How did you come up with the plot for 'Fool's Paradise'?"

"Well, uh . . . what do you mean, exactly?" Maggie asked.

"You know, was it from personal experience or—"

"That's it," Maggie said. "You've hit the button on the head exactly. Personal experience."

Button on the head? Must be an Irish expression, Elizabeth thought. "All right . . . so, how do you get your inspiration as a writer?"

"That's easy. Coffee!" Maggie said. "Lots and lots of coffee."

Elizabeth fiddled with a magnet on the refrigerator. That was odd. She'd read in the biography that Maggie Sullivan, in addition to being a writer, was an expert on tea. She made a point of drinking strong tea every morning before starting to write. Well, maybe she'd changed since coming to this country. Tea wasn't such a big deal in the United States.

Elizabeth decided to move on to her questions specifically about the play. She didn't want to push her luck by asking too many personal questions.

"Maggie? Maybe you could tell me something about county Cork. I want my play to sound and look authentic," Elizabeth said. "Could you give me a few more details about the time and the place? You know, what was county Cork like back then?"

"Er—ah—county Cork, did you say?" Maggie asked, her voice squeaking.

"Right," Elizabeth said.

"Let me see. County Cork, county Cork . . . ah,

you know, it's been a long time since I've been back," Maggie said.

"But you must remember something," Elizabeth said.

"At my age, I'm lucky if I remember my name, some mornings," Maggie said with a nervous cackle. "In fact, I have it written right by my bedside. Maggie O'Sullivan."

"O'Sullivan?" Elizabeth repeated. "But I thought your name was—"

"Ah, what am I saying? Maggie McSullivan!" Maggie laughed, with sort of a low rattle in her throat.

All of a sudden, Elizabeth felt goose bumps on her neck. There was something oddly familiar about that laugh. And that voice . . . it wasn't Irish. Elizabeth was starting to wonder if it even belonged to a woman at all! She didn't know her own name, she didn't know that she drank tea. . . . She'd hedged on the question about county Cork. . . . Elizabeth was talking to someone who didn't know the least thing about Maggie Sullivan!

"Steven!" she shouted into the phone. "How dare you!"

"Ah, no, don't be upset," Steven said in a bad phony accent. "The luck of the green is always with you and—"

"Shut up!" Elizabeth said.

He burst out laughing. "Gotcha!"

"You didn't get me," Elizabeth lied. "And don't

ever call here again!" She slammed down the phone, her eyes brimming with tears. How dare Steven try to fool her like that!

First Jessica was mean to her at lunch—now Steven?

She'd had more than enough of being made fun of. If they thought they could get away with treating her that way, they were wrong. She would have to give them a taste of their own medicine . . . but how?

Maybe I'll start with a taste of sand, she thought. *A mouthful, actually.*

"So what's the plan?" Amy asked as she and Elizabeth coasted to a stop just above Sunset Beach.

"Complete and utter revenge," Elizabeth said, stepping off her bicycle. "This is going to get Jessica back for being so selfish and mean lately, and Steven for thinking he's so great."

"Wow. And you thought it up in the half hour since you called me to meet you here?" Amy asked, putting her bike into the rack and locking it securely.

"What can I say? I was motivated," Elizabeth said. "Ready?"

Amy nodded, and the two of them walked down the steep rocks and onto the sandy beach. "Funny. I don't see the fashion queens here raking up any gold," Amy commented.

"Oh, they're not," Elizabeth said. "Jessica told

me that she and Lila are meeting Rick Hunter at Casey's after school, so I decided to take the opportunity to come here."

"Because . . . you're going to dig for the pot of gold they're so excited about? And steal it from them?" Amy asked.

"No, of course not," Elizabeth said, gazing around the beach. She tried to remember the two X's on the map. She'd had a good five minutes to look at the map, and she had nearly memorized it. "There's no such thing as a pot of gold. Even if there is, it's definitely not buried here, in Sweet Valley. I mean, wouldn't that be kind of hard to believe?"

"Sure," Amy said. "I didn't believe it for a second."

"But Jessica does, and so does Lila," Elizabeth said. "They think there's a pot of gold here only because Steven made them think there's one—just like he made me think I was talking to Maggie Sullivan. Well, guess what. It's time they both learned a lesson about humility."

Amy took a few steps backwards. "Elizabeth, you're scaring me!"

Elizabeth laughed. "Believe me, this isn't going to be scary at all. It's going to be a lot of fun." She opened her small leather backpack. "Wait until you see the stuff I brought." She pulled out a smooth, large, flat white stone.

"What's that for?" Amy asked.

"If Jessica and Lila want to find clues and buried treasure, then they're going to find them," Elizabeth declared, rubbing the stone. She handed it to Amy and pulled out a small note she'd written at home. "When they see this, they're going to think they've hit the jackpot." She handed the note to Amy, with a piece of tape. "Make sure that's taped on, and we'll bury it . . . right over here." She tapped the sand with her foot.

"You've made it this far. You're hot, not cold! Kiss the Blarney stone, and go on to the gold!" Amy read out loud. She burst out laughing. "*Blarney* stone? This thing? Isn't the Blarney stone in Ireland?"

"Sure, but anyone who believes a pot of Irish gold is going to turn up in Sweet Valley will believe anything," Elizabeth said with a smile.

"This is going to be *good*," Amy said, digging a hole for the stone. "I can't wait to see the looks on their faces when they put their lips on this stone." She glanced up at Elizabeth. "We are going to watch them, aren't we? Or did you bring a video camera to put in the tree?"

"I would, if I had one," Elizabeth said. "We'll have to watch it live and in progress." It was really too bad, because a videotape like that would definitely come in handy in the future. Whenever Jessica and Steven started acting superior, she could pop it in the VCR.

"I can't wait," Amy said. She scooped up a few

inches of sand, then placed the stone at the bottom of the hole. She covered it back up, making sure the sand looked smooth and undisturbed.

"Next up, we know that every pot of gold has a key," Elizabeth said, fishing a small key out of her backpack. She'd tied another small note to the key. It contained the second clue to finding the pot of gold.

"Where'd you get that?" Amy asked, brushing off her hands to take the key.

"It's from one of my old diaries," Elizabeth told her. "I threw out the diary, but I still had the key in my jewelry box. It's all rusted and scratched up."

"OK. Excellent. Where should we bury this?"

Elizabeth looked around the beach, trying to recall the map. "I think it goes over there." She pointed to the other end of the beach.

"Man, Jessica and Lila are going to have their work cut out for them," Amy commented as she and Elizabeth walked down the beach along the water.

"Can you see Lila digging?" Elizabeth said, zipping her backpack closed.

"For anything other than cash? No," Amy said. "She'll probably stop as soon as she breaks a nail!"

Elizabeth grinned as she picked a spot and started digging. Once he heard about the buried treasure, Steven would forget all about his barbells and push-ups. He'd get all his exercise digging up Sunset Beach. And Jessica and Lila could quit telling her she didn't know how to dress. The only fashion they'd be wearing for the next few days would be layers and layers of sand!

Joe Howell slapped Steven on the back as they walked into the mall Wednesday afternoon. "Dude, I still can't believe you pulled that practical joke on your sister. If you could have heard your voice—" He started laughing. "You were like someone in a low-budget movie. Like they couldn't hire an Irish actor so they got someone else and—"

"Hey, I thought I was pretty good," Steven said. "Considering I've never even been to Ireland."

"And considering you're not a *woman*." Joe laughed. "I've got an idea. Tomorrow, why don't you show up at the house and pretend to be that writer in person? I can see you in a dress and high heels. A little red lipstick—"

"OK, you can stop now," Steven said. "I get the point. But I don't think I could fool Elizabeth again—even if I wanted to wear a dress, which I don't, thank you very much."

Elizabeth was much too smart to fall for that joke twice. Even though he'd really had her going for a while there, with his phony accent and all he knew about Maggie whatever-her-last-name-was. OK, so it wasn't much, but he'd stretched it to a full three minutes. Poor Elizabeth. She'd sounded so happy!

Maybe now she'd think twice about making fun of him for working out so much. Was it a crime to be in shape? Was it wrong to want to be faster and stronger?

Of course, a guy couldn't exercise twenty-four hours a day. That was why Steven and Joe were headed to Casey's for frozen yogurt shakes. Steven was so hungry from all his exercising that he wanted to get a triple banana split—or two. But *real* athletes didn't eat junk food. Steven would order a frozen yogurt instead.

When they walked into Casey's, Steven couldn't believe his eyes. Jessica and Lila were sitting there with some boys, laughing and talking!

Steven frowned. OK, so that was their natural habitat. But today, they were supposed to be running all over town, searching for buried treasure.

"Order for me, Joe. I have to go take care of Sister II, the sequel," Steven said.

"What are you going to do now? Pretend you're a leprechaun?" Joe teased.

Steven just shook his head and walked over to Jessica's table. "Jessica, I know what you're up to."

She looked up at him, raising an eyebrow. "Excuse me? Are you our waiter?"

Lila giggled.

"You stole my map. Quit pretending you didn't," Steven said.

"Map? What are you talking about?" Jessica asked, her mouth open in surprise.

"The map I found. You took it. Just confess already, I'm getting bored," Steven said.

"You're not the only one." Jessica glared at him, as if he were ruining her entire afternoon.

Steven grinned. Wasn't this what being siblings was all about?

"I didn't take your map. I haven't seen your map, I don't have your map, I don't even know what your dumb map looks like, so even if I fell over it, I wouldn't recognize it!" Jessica said. "Now go away."

"Gladly," Steven said. "But if I find out you had anything to do with its disappearance, you'll be sorry. I need that map! It's important."

"Why, do the old fogies at the hysterical society want it?" Jessica asked.

"Historical society," Steven corrected her. "Sure, they want it. They told me it's probably authentic, that it might date back a hundred years or more. And they also told me it could be valuable in lots of other ways. Which is why I want it back . . . *now.*"

Steven thought he saw Jessica's eyes light up, but she kept her cool.

"Sorry." Jessica shrugged. "No can do. Now get lost. My ice cream's practically been melted by all your hot air."

She and Lila started laughing.

"Good one, Jessica!" a boy with blond hair told Jessica. Steven decided he must be that Rick guy Jessica kept talking about.

Steven stepped away from the table and went over to meet up with Joe. Mission accomplished!

*   *   *

"My big brother can be such a pain," Jessica said.

"Well, you got him pretty good," Rick remarked.

"I did, didn't I?" Jessica was smiling at Rick, who was sitting across the table from her, when she felt a tap on her leg. She turned to Lila, who was sitting next to her. "What?" she asked. She hated being interrupted just when Rick was starting to notice how wonderful she was.

"I need to . . . powder my nose," Lila said. "Come with me."

Jessica frowned at her. Why did Lila always pick the wrong times to have to go to the bathroom? "OK," she sighed. "Excuse us. We'll be right back."

She followed Lila into the girls' room. Once the door swung shut, Lila grabbed Jessica's arm. Her face was pale.

"What's the matter? Are you going to be sick?" Jessica jumped back in alarm.

"No. But you're going to be sorry if we don't hit Sunset Beach as soon as we can," Lila said. "Did you hear how serious Steven was? I mean, he's really upset about losing his map. And he said it has all kinds of value."

"So?" Jessica said. "It's not like we're going to give it *back* to him just because he's upset he lost it."

"No, but he could steal it back from you," Lila pointed out. "That's why we have to make sure *we* get the gold—and *soon*. Steven can't find the map. He can't follow us tomorrow after school when we go there. . . ." She stopped, her face scrunched in concentration. "Do you think maybe we should tie him up until this is all over?"

"Lila! We're not cowboys," Jessica said. "Listen. I'm going to sleep with that treasure map under my pillow. Steven won't get it back. And we'll make sure no one's following us."

"So tomorrow, it's a date. As soon as school lets out, we head for Sunset Beach," Lila whispered, even though no one else was in the bathroom.

"But what if Rick asks me out again? I mean, we could go to Sunset Beach a little later . . . in the evening or something. Or this weekend!" Jessica said excitedly. "We'd have lots more time and—"

"Forget it," Lila said. "I don't care if Rick asks you to marry him tomorrow afternoon. You're going to say no."

"Well, sure. I mean, who wants to get married on a Thursday?" Jessica said. "Totally tacky." She put her arm around Lila's shoulders. "Come on, let's get back to the table. It might be the last time we ever come here, and I want to enjoy it."

"The last time?" Lila asked.

"Sure," Jessica said. "If I find a pot of gold, I'm having my sundaes delivered."

"If *we* find it, you mean," Lila said.

"We. Right. Of course," Jessica said. "So wear grubby clothes tomorrow, OK?" she told Lila. "We'll have a lot of hard digging to do."

Lila wrinkled her nose. "How grubby?"

"Think sweatshirt," Jessica said. "Old sweat-shirt. And shorts."

Lila looked down at her cute pink-and-black checked miniskirt and pink baby T-shirt. "I think I'll bring that stuff in a bag and change after school. That is, if I *own* any old sweatshirts."

Jessica rolled her eyes. Why she was letting someone as rich as Lila in on her pot of gold was a total mystery to her. In her opinion, friendship was completely overrated!

Nine

Elizabeth flipped through the telephone directory Thursday morning while she ate breakfast. So far, she'd found only three M. Sullivans listed, and each one she'd called had turned out to be named Maureen Sullivan.

But even though she felt a little frustrated, she wasn't upset. She was glad she hadn't let Steven's stupid practical joke get to her. And now that she'd set up her own joke, it was a lot easier to concentrate on more important things—like finding Maggie Sullivan. The *real* Maggie Sullivan.

I wouldn't be surprised if Steven took out a listing with the phone company, just to trick me again.

She'd called directory assistance the night before, but all the operator would tell her was that there was no listed number under that name. Elizabeth stared out the window. Was there any way she could at least get Maggie Sullivan's address?

Just then the telephone rang. Elizabeth eyed it suspiciously. Steven had already left for school. What if he was at a phone booth, calling to trick her again?

"Elizabeth!" Jessica shouted downstairs. "It's for you!"

"Is it a woman with an Irish accent?" Elizabeth yelled back.

"No," Jessica said.

"Oh. OK, I'll take it," Elizabeth said. She lifted the receiver off the hook. "Hello?"

"Hi there, Elizabeth. This is Gwen Bramblyhedge, vice president of the Southern California Writers' association," a woman said politely.

"Oh—hi," Elizabeth said. She tried not to get too excited. After all, Steven could fake a high, sweet voice—or have one of his friends do it. "Thanks for calling me back."

"My pleasure," Gwen said. "Listen, I just came into the office and heard your message. We're closed Wednesdays, and that's why no one got back to you yesterday. But you sounded urgent, so I wanted to call right away."

"Thanks, I appreciate it," Elizabeth said. So far, Gwen sounded perfectly genuine. She had to be a real person—Steven wasn't clever enough to make up a name like hers anyway. Elizabeth crossed her fingers, hoping she was about to find out how to get in touch with her favorite writer.

"However, I'm afraid I've got some bad news for you," Gwen continued. "I have absolutely no information regarding Maggie Sullivan."

Elizabeth's heart sank. "None? None at all?"

"All I can tell you is that she was a member of our association years ago, when she first relocated here. But we haven't seen her, or heard from her, in quite a long time," Gwen said. "I'm so sorry I can't help you."

"Do you have an old phone number for her or an old address?" Elizabeth asked.

"Nothing that still works," Gwen said. "Believe me, we like to keep track of our members. Especially one as well known as Maggie Sullivan. But we can't force anyone to come forward."

"No, I know," Elizabeth said. "Well, thanks for calling and telling me."

"You're welcome. I wish I had better news," Gwen said. "Good-bye!"

Elizabeth hung up the phone with a sigh. How was she ever going to find someone who didn't want to be found?

Jessica turned the map one way. Then she turned it another way. "*I* don't know. Here, you look at it."

Lila pushed her sand-covered hair back from her face. Then she grabbed the map out of Jessica's hand. "There has to be some more information. We can't dig up the whole beach—unless we get a steam shovel. And I am not going to be the human steam shovel."

Jessica frowned at her. Was she kidding? Lila was more like the human steam *fork*—with one tine. She'd dug about a tenth as much sand as Jessica had.

Why didn't I ask Elizabeth to go in on this with me instead of Lila? Jessica wondered. *Elizabeth would have done her half of the work—and probably even more,* Jessica thought with a sigh.

"I think we should go over to that side of the beach," Lila said, pointing in the opposite direction.

"But the small *X*, which must be clue number one, is closer to the tree, which would be on *this* side," Jessica argued. "We can't dig up the big *X* first. The pot of gold could disappear!"

"Like it hasn't already disappeared," Lila scoffed. "You know, maybe we're not at the right place. Maybe we should go home, study the map a little longer—"

"Lila! We've only been digging for an hour," Jessica said. "We can't give up yet!"

"I guess not," Lila said. She looked around the beach, and at a couple of swimmers who were jogging out of the ocean. "Maybe we could ask them to help us!"

"Lila, we've been over this," Jessica said. "We can't have anyone else help us. There's no way we're letting someone else take our gold."

"OK, OK! Really, Jessica, it was just a suggestion. You don't have to bite my head off," Lila said.

"Well. Maybe I wouldn't feel so angry, if you'd just start digging faster," Jessica said.

"Me? Why should I dig faster?" Lila protested.

"Because you've barely moved two grains of sand since we got here!" Jessica cried.

"Well, it's not my fault you didn't bring a shovel," Lila said.

"What was I going to do, put it in my locker? You're the one who made us come straight from school," Jessica shot back. She cleaned some sand out from underneath her fingernails. "Look. This isn't getting us anywhere. We've got to keep searching right here. Are you going to help me or not?"

Lila kicked some sand around, burying her toes, then uncovering them. "I guess I can help."

Gee, thanks, Jessica thought, getting back down on her hands and knees. *Don't do me any favors! I'm only the one who told you all about the magic pot of gold in the first place!*

"They look like they're arguing." Amy adjusted the focus on the binoculars.

"That sounds right," Elizabeth said, nodding. "An hour of work . . . a ten-minute break to argue . . . they're right on schedule!" She giggled.

She and Amy had followed Jessica and Lila to Sunset Beach after school, and they were perched on the grassy slope above, just out of sight. So far, Elizabeth was really enjoying herself. She and Amy had brought a couple sodas and some cookies. It was like having a picnic with free entertainment.

"I can't believe they haven't found anything yet," Amy said. "Do you think we missed the spot?"

Elizabeth shook her head. "No, I think they missed it. From what I can see, they're about ten feet off from where we buried the rock."

"Rock? You mean Blarney stone, don't you?" Amy laughed. "And how can you remember where we buried it anyway?"

"See that piece of driftwood? It's right in front of there," Elizabeth said, pointing.

Amy looked through the binoculars again. "Uh-oh. They're stopping again."

"Here, let me see," Elizabeth said. Amy handed her the binoculars. Elizabeth checked out Jessica first. Her sister was flopped down on the beach, on her back, stretching her arms over her head. She was making a face. She seemed to be in pain.

Lila was standing over her, crumpling the treasure map into a small ball. Then, with a final look of disgust at Jessica, she turned and headed for the water. She was about to throw the map into the ocean!

"Come on, Amy, we've got to go down there," Elizabeth said, putting the binoculars down on the picnic blanket. "They're about to give up!" Elizabeth couldn't let that happen. It would ruin her whole plan!

* * *

"I knew you'd try to steal the gold. I knew it," Lila said when Elizabeth and Amy walked down onto the beach. She was standing at the edge of the ocean, and the map was still crumpled in her hand.

"I'm not here to steal anything," Elizabeth said. "What are you doing with the map?"

"Well, I was going to throw it into the ocean," Lila said angrily. "But then I realized I might kill a fish or something so I decided to find a trash can instead. But now that you're here, forget it! I'm holding onto it."

Elizabeth glanced at Jessica, who was still flat on her back. She really looked terrible. Her hair was matted down by sand, and her clothes were sticking to her. "Are you OK?" she asked her sister.

"I'm fine. My arms are a little sore, that's all," Jessica said. "So what are you doing here?" She grimaced as she sat up.

"We're not here to steal anything, if that's what you're worried about," Elizabeth said.

"We were on a bike ride and we saw you guys," Amy explained. "We just wondered how it was going, that's all."

"Do the words *waste of time* mean anything to you?" Lila grumbled.

"It's not a waste of time," Jessica said, rubbing her shoulder. "It's just taking longer than we thought. But we know where the first clue is. We'll find it sooner or later."

Elizabeth nodded. "Just keep a positive attitude." She started circling the area in front of the driftwood, kicking the sand around. "I mean, eventually you have to come across—*whoa!*" She stubbed her toe against the stone and sprawled onto the beach, hands first.

"Watch it," Lila said. "You're disturbing our dig area." She sounded like a scientist.

"Are you all right?" Amy asked, rushing to Elizabeth's side.

"I'm OK. I just tripped on this dumb rock, that's all." Elizabeth tried to keep a straight face as she lifted the stone out of the sand.

"What's that?" Amy asked. "Is that a *note* on that rock?"

"Must be a love letter," Elizabeth joked, lifting the small piece of paper.

Jessica jumped to her feet. "It's the clue! Lila, it's our first clue! We found it!" She ran over to Elizabeth.

"Well, technically, I found it," Elizabeth began, "or rather, my big toe found it—"

"But it *belongs* to us," Jessica said, greedily grabbing the rock from Elizabeth's hand. She stared at the piece of paper, her eyes growing wide with excitement.

Elizabeth snuck a glance at Amy, biting her lip to keep from smiling. So far, so good.

"Lila, check this out!" Jessica squealed. "You've made it this far. You're *hot*, not cold! Kiss the Blarney stone, and go on to the gold!" She gave the stone a big kiss, then held it up in the air striumphantly. "A Blarney stone! Ireland! The gold!" she yelled.

"My turn!" Lila cried, taking the stone from her. She kissed it about a dozen times. Her lips were covered with sand. "Thhhpt," she sputtered.

"Well, see you guys later," Jessica said. "We've got work to do!" She ran to the other end of the beach.

Lila was right behind her, kissing the stone again and again as she ran.

Elizabeth watched them, her arms folded with satisfaction. "Well, that's one thing I never thought I'd see. Lila Fowler falling in love with a stone."

Jessica dug as fast as she could, flinging sand behind her. She had to admit that even Lila was digging pretty quickly. They moved down the beach in a straight line, then went the other way. Jessica wanted to make sure they covered every foot of land that was anywhere near that second X.

Go on to the gold, she repeated in her head. *You're hot, not cold. Go on to the gold.* She felt a little like she was in a trance.

Every other minute, Lila took the Blarney stone out of her beach bag, kissed it for luck, then put it back.

Jessica glanced over her shoulder. The sun was almost about to set. The sky was orange-red, and the ocean had lost its blue hue. "We've got to find it today," she muttered. "But if we don't find it before it's dark—"

"There's no way I can stay here once the sun

goes down," Lila said, pausing for a minute. "My dad expects me home."

"I should get home too. OK. We'll look for five more minutes," Jessica said. She glanced back over at the piece of driftwood, where they'd found the Blarney stone. The second X was supposed to be in a straight line from there.

"I think we're a little off course," Jessica said, scooting backward on her heels. "We should find it right about here." She started digging. She kept digging. She was starting to feel like this was getting pointless again.

Then, all of a sudden, her fingers touched something small—and it felt like metal! "Lila, I got a piece of gold!" she yelled, yanking her hand out of the sand.

But what her fingers were clutching wasn't gold at all. It was a key—a small silver key that looked like it had been buried for years. Attached to it was a small note.

"You've found clue number two, you've got the right angle. The pot of gold can be found, if you make a perfect triangle!" Jessica read, her heart pounding.

"A triangle?" Lila said.

"A triangle!" Jessica said, jumping up. "See, it was a straight line from clue one to here . . . so if we make a triangle, the pot of gold would be . . ."

"Six feet into the ocean?" Lila guessed.

"No. Back that way—right there!" Jessica pointed

to a spot just underneath the grassy slope overlooking the beach. "Lila, we're going to get the gold!" She slapped Lila's palm in a high five.

"We'll come back tomorrow, right after school," Lila said.

"Tomorrow?" Jessica said. "But—it's right there, and we're already here, and—"

"And it's practically getting dark, and in another half hour we won't be able to see a thing," Lila argued. "Plus my dad will get mad at me, and ground me, so I won't even be able to come back tomorrow, or do anything with the gold once we get it."

"How big a pot do you think it is?" Jessica asked.

"I don't know," Lila said. "Why?"

"Well, if it's not that big, maybe I could carry it all by myself," Jessica said. "You could go home, I'll stay here a little longer, and—"

"No way," Lila said, pulling Jessica behind her as she headed toward the boardwalk. "You're not doing this without me."

Jessica sighed. She had to admit, Lila had a point. Digging in the dark didn't make much sense. She'd probably pull up a pot of oysters and think it was gold.

But when they came back Friday afternoon, Jessica was going to be ready. Her lifetime of happiness was only twenty-four hours away.

Ten

◇

"Where have you been?" Mr. Wakefield asked when Jessica walked into the house late Thursday evening.

"I don't think we need to ask," Mrs. Wakefield said. "Look at her! You were at the beach all this time? What on earth were you doing?"

Steven started coughing. It was all he could do not to burst out laughing. Jessica had so much sand stuck to her, she looked like a piece of chicken that had just been coated with seasoning before going in the oven.

So she did get the clue about Sunset Beach after all, he thought, feeling satisfied. Of course, he'd made it cute and clever—but not too clever. The point was to make Jessica think she was on the trail of gold as soon as possible. The sooner she started looking for it, the sooner she'd be completely miserable.

But there was one major problem. Jessica didn't look unhappy at all! She was actually *grinning*. Jessica, who couldn't stand to have one hair out of place—and her hair was now as clumpy and sandy as stranded seaweed. What was the deal?

"So what were you doing there this whole time? You missed dinner. We were worried about you," Mr. Wakefield said.

Jessica stood in the doorway to the dining room. "I don't want to come in. I'd better take a shower first. But Lila and I went to the beach. Remember, I told you this morning I was going to be home late."

"So what happened to you?" Mrs. Wakefield asked. "You look like you were buried in sand."

"No, *I* wasn't." Jessica smiled mischievously, with a quick glance at Elizabeth.

"What does that mean?" Steven asked. This whole happy-go-lucky routine of hers was really starting to get on his nerves.

"Oh, uh . . . Lila. Lila was buried in the sand. We were playing . . . beach volleyball. With some friends—you know, the Unicorns against the—"

"Trolls?" Steven joked.

Jessica stuck out her tongue at him. "You're just jealous, because we had so much fun."

"Not exactly," Steven grumbled.

"So who won?" Elizabeth asked.

"Oh, they did," Jessica said. "I got so sandy because, you know, I kept diving for the ball. But we lost, so Lila got buried in the sand because she was our team captain, and that was the bet and everything. Well, gotta go shower. Save me some food, I'm starving!"

Steven watched as she disappeared up the stairs. What was going on? She had to have been lying about playing beach volleyball. But if she had tried to make sense of that map . . . why wasn't she totally frustrated and mad at the world? It wasn't like Jessica to take defeat lightly.

"Come on, Steven. Let's clear the dishes," Elizabeth said.

"OK." Steven didn't have the energy to argue that he hated clearing the table. He picked up his mother's plate and followed Elizabeth into the kitchen in a daze.

"Steven," Elizabeth whispered, grabbing his sleeve as he put the dirty plates into the dishwasher.

"What? I'm not doing it right?" Steven asked.

Elizabeth shook her head. "Not that. I have something important to tell you."

Steven leaned against the counter. Important? He considered mentioning that he doubted his dweeby sister could tell him anything that would qualify as important, but he decided he was just a little bit curious. "OK, shoot."

"Well, it's about your map. The treasure map you found at the park," Elizabeth said. "Remember how you couldn't find it the next day, and you thought you'd lost it?"

Steven nodded. "Sure."

"You didn't lose it," Elizabeth said with a serious expression. "Jessica *stole* it."

Steven bit back a grin. So his plan was working! "*No*," he gasped.

"Yes, it's true. And what's more, she's already very, very close to finding the treasure. I saw her at the beach this afternoon. She found the first clue—a rock with a note attached to it. And she was about to find the second when I left," Elizabeth said in a whisper. "After she does that—well, she's practically found the pot of gold. And that's *your* pot of gold, Steven. You'd better check it out before it's too late!"

Steven widened his eyes. What did she mean, Jessica found the first clue? The map was a fake, wasn't it? Steven and Joe had drawn the map together. Unless Joe knew something he didn't . . .

"Well?" Elizabeth asked. "What are you going to do about it?"

"I—I don't know," Steven said.

"If I were you, I'd get to Sunset Beach tomorrow afternoon, after school," Elizabeth said. "That's what I'd do. Because if it were my map, I sure wouldn't let someone else get the treasure. That wouldn't be fair."

"No," Steven said slowly, his pulse starting to race. "It wouldn't be fair at all!" If Jessica was about to find something valuable, he wanted in on it!

*   *   *

"Where did you get that?"

"From the gardener, where else?" Lila replied, carrying the shovel on her shoulder.

"It's a good thing you did." Jessica massaged her arm muscles. "I'm so sore from yesterday, I don't even think I can move one ounce of sand."

She stepped off the boardwalk onto the beach. Sunset Beach was starting to feel a little too familiar. If they didn't find the gold that afternoon, she'd have to spend her whole weekend there, digging her way around people's playpens and towels, sweating under the hot sun.

"Just think," Lila said, propping the shovel in the sand and leaning against it. "If we find the gold today, we're going to have the most major shopping spree of our *lives* tomorrow."

Jessica grabbed the shovel from her and started running. "Pot of gold, here we come!" she yelled. Sometimes, all you needed was the right inspiration.

Using the shovel, she drew a line in the sand, connecting the two spots where they'd found the stone and the key. *Keystone . . . that must mean something in Irish folklore. Like jackpot!* Jessica thought excitedly. Lila followed her as she drew two lines going straight out from the clue locations.

"When these two lines intersect, that will be a perfect triangle," Jessica said, concentrating on keeping the lines as straight as possible.

"So you were paying attention in math yesterday," Lila teased.

"I guess Ms. Wyler was right when she said geometry would count in real life," Jessica said with a laugh. "She had no idea how *much*."

Finally, Jessica reached the spot where the two lines crossed. She marked a giant X in the sand. "Lila? Are you ready?"

Lila nodded eagerly.

"Stand back," Jessica warned. As soon as Lila was out of the way, Jessica pushed the shovel into the sand as far as it would go. She stomped on the shovel with her right foot, then pulled a giant heap of sand out. She grunted, tossing the sand to one side, then pushed the shovel in again.

"Man, this is exhausting," she complained to Lila, hoping Lila would get the hint and volunteer to take over.

"It looks exhausting," Lila observed. "Good thing you're so strong!"

Jessica glared at her. "Well, I might *look* strong," she said. "But I don't *feel* strong."

"Think of it this way—you're building great muscle tone!" Lila said cheerfully.

Jessica grunted, digging in again. She didn't *want* muscle tone. She wanted help!

"Everything all right? Can I help you?" a male voice behind her asked.

"No, thanks, we've got it covered." Jessica looked over her shoulder.

She almost fell into the small hole she'd dug. It was Steven!

"You've got it covered, have you?" he said in a snide voice. "Actually, it looks like you've almost got it *un*covered!"

"It? What do you mean, *it?*" Lila asked.

"Lila and I are just, uh, fixing the spot where we played volleyball yesterday. We kind of tore up the beach and the lifeguard said we should—"

"Forget it," Steven said. "I'm not buying your beach volleyball story anymore. I know what you're doing. Elizabeth told me how you stole my treasure map. And you're here digging for something that obviously belongs to *me*." He reached for the shovel. "Now, if you don't mind, I'd like to find *my* pot of gold."

"*Your* pot of gold? Since when?" Jessica replied, holding the shovel out of his reach. She felt her face burn with rage. How dare Elizabeth break her promise and blab to Steven!

"Who was here yesterday, finding all the clues? Who figured out it was at Sunset Beach? Who dug up half the sand on this beach looking for it?" Lila demanded. "We did."

More like I did! Jessica thought. Still, Lila had a good point. "Lila's right," she told Steven. "You lost track of the treasure map, and that means you don't deserve the gold. Everyone knows that. It's part of the legend, OK? And—and—" She struggled to think of more reasons why the treasure wasn't Steven's. "And not only do you have to follow the clues in order, *but* the same people who start digging have to finish digging. Or else the pot of gold will disappear. It says so right on the map."

"I don't think so," Steven said.

Lila shrugged. "Well, it does."

"Listen," Steven said fiercely. "You guys are lucky I haven't charged you with breaking and entering. You went into my room and took something that was locked up. That's against the law, you know."

Jessica flipped her hair over her shoulder. "What are you going to do, take me to The People's Court? You don't have any proof."

"Yes I do," Steven retorted. "And here she comes right now." He pointed to the boardwalk. Elizabeth and Amy were heading their way.

Jessica stared at her sister as she marched toward them with a smile on her face. Who was she to look so happy after what she did? Didn't she know the least thing about keeping a secret? "This is all your fault!" Jessica yelled as soon as Elizabeth was within earshot.

"Me? What did I do?" Elizabeth asked.

"You told Steven I took his dumb map," Jessica said. "Even after you swore you'd keep it a secret. How could you?"

"Well, he—I—," Elizabeth stammered.

"I suppose you were both thinking you could come down here and take home some gold," Jessica said, her hands on her hips. "Well, think again. This belongs to me and Lila."

"This? You mean you found it already?" Amy asked, looking around.

"No, we didn't find it already," Lila said. "Because we keep being so rudely interrupted!"

"So let's get going," Steven said.

"Let's?" Jessica repeated.

"You and me. Oh, and Lila too, I guess," Steven sighed. "It was my map, and you found the clues. So we're even. We'll just have to split three ways."

"But—but—," Jessica tried to protest, but she really couldn't think of anything to say. Steven *had* found the map in the first place. Besides, if he helped, he could do most of the digging. "Well, I don't know, Lila. What do you think?"

"I think this is a horrible development." She glared at Elizabeth. "But what else can we do?"

Jessica handed Steven the shovel. "Well, at least all that weight lifting wasn't for nothing. Start digging."

"Gee, Elizabeth," Lila said. "Sorry, but it looks like you're the only one in the family who won't be getting any gold."

Elizabeth frowned. "Of all the luck."

Jessica smiled. Even though she hated having to share with Steven, she was glad Elizabeth had learned her lesson. If you didn't keep your word, if you couldn't be trusted . . . you had to pay the price!

Eleven

"Look at them. They're worse than a couple of golden retrievers," Amy joked.

"You're right," Elizabeth said. "I've never seen Lila work so hard before."

Elizabeth couldn't help being proud of her revenge plan. She was waiting until Jessica, Lila, and Steven were completely worn out and dirty. When they started drawing the *other* end of the triangle, and digging under six-foot waves, maybe then she'd tell them the truth. There was no buried treasure. There never had been one. There wasn't going to be any magic pot of gold.

Then she'd take out her camera and quickly snap a picture of their shocked, horrified faces.

Steven and Jessica would never believe Elizabeth could pull off this kind of practical joke. In fact,

Elizabeth was a little surprised at her own knack for vengeance. *They shouldn't have been so mean to me,* she reasoned. *That's the only reason I'm doing this.*

It had been a lot of fun, so far. But as rewarding as the whole experience was, Elizabeth felt a tiny twinge of guilt as she saw drops of sweat rolling off Jessica's face. She hadn't really expected her twin to search so intensely—for two days in a row!

I'll buy her some bubble bath tomorrow, Elizabeth decided. *She can soak her aching muscles.*

"I've found the spot!" Jessica cried suddenly. "I can just feel it. I have goose bumps and everything."

"You've had goose bumps eight times in the last fifteen minutes," Lila said. "I'm starting to think you're coming down with a fever."

"Either that or a rash," Steven commented, staring down at the sand.

"I'm serious, you guys," Jessica said. "Help me dig, please? Right here!" She pointed to a spot on the sand.

Steven sighed. "Might as well try here as anywhere."

"Wait a second—I've got something!" Jessica cried. "It's small, and there's a string . . ."

Elizabeth took her compact camera out of her pocket and held it up in front of her eye. In just a few seconds, Jessica was going to pull a long strand of seaweed out of the sand—and she'd capture it on film!

Jessica pulled her arm out of the deep hole. In

her hand, she was clutching a string—attached to a small, purple velveteen bag that looked like it had seen better days.

What's that? Elizabeth wondered. She hadn't planted anything in that spot. The bag looked ratty and worn. *Someone probably dropped it here a long time ago. It's not worth anything,* Elizabeth decided.

"Hold on—there's something inside," Jessica muttered, trying to undo the tie.

Elizabeth's finger was poised on the photo button. No doubt the bag was full of sand. She could hardly wait to see Jessica's face.

"You guys aren't going to believe this!" Jessica said. She pulled a piece of jewelry out of the bag. "Gold!"

"Gold?" Elizabeth was so surprised, she snapped the picture—and keeled over, face first, onto the beach. What was gold doing there?

"Gold?" Steven repeated.

"Gold!" Lila declared.

"Huh?" Amy asked.

Elizabeth struggled to her feet. "But I didn't bury that in the sand!"

Lila, Jessica, and Steven turned to her, their eyes flashing. With a sinking heart, Elizabeth realized she'd said a little too much.

"Then what exactly *did* you bury?" Jessica demanded.

Elizabeth shrugged nervously. "Not much. Only . . . everything else?"

*   *   *

Steven shook his head. He couldn't believe it, now that he'd heard the whole story. Elizabeth was becoming more like Jessica every day. That was definitely a trend that needed to be nipped in the bud. Like, yesterday, if not sooner.

"So you came down here and hid all these clues, just to make us look like fools," Lila concluded.

"Pretty much," Elizabeth admitted.

"Elizabeth! That's a horrible thing to do," Jessica said. "And *you*." She pointed at Amy. "You helped, didn't you?"

Amy nodded sheepishly.

"But why?" Steven asked. "I mean, why would you go to so much trouble?"

"Gee, I don't know. Why would you go to so much trouble to pretend to be Maggie Sullivan?" Elizabeth retorted.

"Well, yeah, but—that was different," Steven said. "That was funny."

Elizabeth stuck out her tongue at him.

"OK, so I can see why you'd want to get Steven back, but what did *I* ever do to you?" Jessica asked.

Elizabeth folded her arms. "Oh, nothing. Except act like the greediest, most selfish—"

Jessica gasped. "Me? You're talking about me? But Elizabeth, I *told* you I'd give you a twenty-dollar bill. Of course, that was for keeping my secret. But since you blabbed to Steven, looks like twenty cents is more in line."

"See? That's exactly what I'm talking about," Elizabeth argued.

"Girls, girls. The past is the past. It's just like we said before, Elizabeth. You and Amy can't have any of the gold, no matter where or why we found it," Steven declared. "Let me see that necklace."

"It's called a locket," Jessica told him.

"Who cares? Whatever it is, it looks valuable." Steven took the necklace from Jessica.

"See if you can get it open," Lila said. "But be careful, it's probably an antique locket."

Steven fiddled with the locket. Finally it popped open. There wasn't anything inside but an inscription. "To Maggie. Love, Patrick," he read.

Elizabeth gasped. "Really? It says that?"

"No, I made it up," Steven said, rolling his eyes. "Look for yourself!" He held the locket in front of her nose, not allowing her to touch it.

"Check it out," Jessica said. "There's a piece of paper in here too." She pulled out a small, light green card. "Maggie Sullivan," she read out loud. "Residing in the city of Sweet Valley at—"

"Sweet Valley?" Elizabeth cried. "She lives right here in Sweet Valley?"

"Who does?" Lila asked.

"Maggie Sullivan!" Elizabeth exclaimed, beaming.

"This is great, Elizabeth," Amy said. "You've been looking all over for her."

"So." Steven looked at Elizabeth. "You're excited about something, are you? You think you found something special? Well, so did we—until we found out you set us up! And guess what. You're not going to get Maggie Sullivan's address—not from us!"

"But—but—," Elizabeth protested. "I was the one who—"

"You're the one who tricked us into thinking we'd find a pot of gold," Lila filled in.

"That wasn't me, that was Steven!" Elizabeth said. She pointed at her brother. "He's the one who drew the phony map in the first place."

Jessica's jaw dropped. "*You* drew it?"

Steven shrugged. "Well, yeah, but—"

"No wonder the pot of gold looked like a pot of coffee," Jessica grumbled.

"Well, what difference does that make now?" Steven asked. "I mean, if I *hadn't* drawn the map, we wouldn't have found this locket."

"Which might be worth something," Lila added, her eyes sparkling.

"You're going to return it to her, aren't you? You're not going to just sell it and cash in, are you?" Elizabeth asked.

"Please. Some of us aren't as heartless as you," Jessica said. "Come on, Lila and Steven, let's go."

"But you guys," Elizabeth pleaded. "You can't go see Maggie Sullivan without me. You don't even know anything about her!"

Steven dangled the locket from his fingers. "You know, somehow I don't think Maggie Sullivan's going to care how much we know about her. We have her gold locket, after all. I think that's enough."

"Ooh, maybe she'll give us a reward!" Jessica said excitedly. "That locket probably has lots of sentimental value."

"Are you—are you going right now?" Elizabeth asked, trailing after them.

"Elizabeth, please. That's our business," Lila said in a haughty tone. "Just like being an utter jerk was your business."

"We might go today. . . . We might go tomorrow. . . . Who knows?" Steven said with a shrug. "But don't worry. When we do go, we'll be sure to tell Maggie Sullivan you said hi." Then he, Lila, and Jessica burst out laughing.

Twelve

"She's not behind us, is she?" Jessica asked Steven.

"Nope. The only one behind us is Lila," Steven told her.

"Good." Jessica switched gears as she pedaled uphill toward Whippoorwill Lane on Saturday morning. Good thing Maggie Sullivan lived so far from the Wakefields' house. Elizabeth would have a hard time finding her. It was odd that Elizabeth hadn't been at home, waiting for them to leave so she could follow them. Jessica almost wished Elizabeth had tried to spy on them. She would have sent her in the absolute wrong direction!

Imagine Elizabeth, pulling a trick like that on us. She still couldn't get over it. *Was I acting that greedy and selfish about finding the gold?* Jessica wondered briefly.

Fortunately, she didn't have to dwell on the question long. A large mailbox on the right-hand side of the road was marked 711 Whippoorwill Lane in purple script. "This is it," she told Steven.

"I wonder if she still lives here," Steven mused as they turned and started pedaling down the long, shaded driveway.

"She would have to live at the top of a hill," Lila panted, coming up behind them. "Writers. They're so weird."

"I think it's beautiful. Totally romantic," Jessica observed, admiring the secluded spot full of bright wildflowers and tangled vines. *Wait until I tell Elizabeth about this*, she thought.

Then she remembered she wasn't supposed to tell her twin anything about the whole experience of meeting Maggie Sullivan. She'd promised Steven that they'd hold out on Elizabeth as long as possible, so she'd really suffer.

Despite herself, Jessica felt the slightest twinge of her least favorite emotion as she saw the small white house with green shutters—guilt. *Elizabeth should be the one seeing this*, she thought briefly. *Well, too bad she blew her chance.*

"I guess you could get a lot of writing done up here," Steven said, getting off his bike and leaning it against the front stairs. "It's quiet."

"Peaceful," Jessica added.

"Boring," Lila said, wiping a cobweb she'd ridden through off her cheek. "She doesn't even have a pool."

"So? Not everyone has to have a pool," Jessica said. She felt like she needed to defend Maggie, since Elizabeth wasn't there to do it. "Maybe she's too busy writing great stuff to go swimming. Did you ever think of that?"

"Sometimes it's more important to have a good tan than to write a good book," Lila muttered under her breath. "Did you ever think of that?"

Jessica ignored her. She walked up the front steps and knocked lightly on the door. She felt nervous. It was strange to show up at someone's house when you didn't know them at all.

She thought she heard someone moving inside the house. A few seconds later, the door opened, revealing a short older woman with white hair and tiny round silver glasses. She was wearing corduroy pants, a white blouse, and a green cardigan sweater that brought out her green eyes.

Jessica took a deep breath. "Hi, my name's Jessica Wakefield. This is my friend Lila, and my brother, Steven. Sorry to come by without calling, but we couldn't find your phone number, and—look, I'm babbling. We just wanted to give you this." Jessica held out the small gold locket. "That is, if it's yours. Are you Maggie Sullivan?"

The woman took off her glasses and reached for the locket. "I—I am," she said, her voice full of emotion. "Where did you find this?"

"On Sunset Beach," Jessica said. "It's yours, isn't it?"

"I . . . I cannot believe it," she said with a fairly strong Irish accent. "I never thought I'd see this again." She pressed the locket to her heart and looked at Jessica, her eyes filling with tears. "I don't know what to say. I cannot thank you enough! Please, come in!"

"Did you hear that?" Lila whispered, walking into the house behind Jessica. "She said she can't thank us enough. That sounds promising, doesn't it?"

Jessica shrugged. At the moment, getting a reward for bringing the locket back was the last thing on her mind. She was too busy thinking of how touched Maggie Sullivan seemed by the locket. *And Elizabeth thought we were going to sell it at a pawn shop or something. Please!* Jessica was much more considerate than that. She enjoyed returning lost things to people and seeing how grateful they were to her.

Of course, Jessica wouldn't say no to a reward, if Mrs. Sullivan offered. That would be rude.

"It's shortbread," Mrs. Sullivan said. "Scottish, not Irish, but that's the best I could do on short notice." She smiled. "Maybe I should call it short notice shortbread."

"Thanks, Mrs. Sullivan," Steven said. "This looks great."

"Ah, you're welcome. But do me a favor and call me Maggie," she replied. "Whenever I hear Mrs. Sullivan, I think you must be talking to someone else. Can you imagine the day when somebody comes up to you and says, 'How do you do, Mr. Wakefield'?"

"No—definitely not!" Steven laughed and reached for a piece of shortbread, his hand shaking slightly. He'd been talking to Maggie for only five minutes, but already he felt like a heel for ever trying to pretend to be someone as nice and genuine as she was. It was almost like making fun of his grandmother.

He looked around the living room, at all the fine prints and interesting photos of Ireland on the wall. Most of the furniture was antique. In the hallway, he'd spotted several framed pictures of Maggie with different famous people—movie stars, even an ex-president. OK, so maybe she was a little more well known than he'd thought.

"Now, is everyone all set?" Maggie asked.

"Please—sit down," Steven said. "You really don't need to wait on us."

"Oh, but I do," Maggie said, taking a seat in an old wooden rocking chair. "I don't even know what to say, I'm so grateful to all of you." She took a sip of iced tea. "But tell me, how in the world did you ever find my locket? I must have lost it . . . oh, ten years ago. It was quite sad. I wore that locket every day of my life—until the day I lost it."

"Well, it's kind of a long story," Jessica said, nibbling at a piece of shortbread. "You probably don't want to hear it all."

"I'd love to hear the whole story," Maggie said. "I'm sure it's very entertaining."

"A little too entertaining, actually," Lila commented. "It's more like . . . silly and ridiculous."

"Ooh. This sounds good," Maggie said, setting down her glass on a small end table. "Should I get my notebook? I'm always looking for new ideas!"

"It's not really a *good* idea," Jessica said. "But here goes. It all started when I had this assignment for school. I had to write a paper about Irish legends."

"Oh, dear. Was I in the book? I hope I'm not so old that I'm considered a legend!" Maggie said, her hand on her throat.

Steven shook his head. "No, it's nothing like that!"

"The part I was reading had a story about a magical pot of gold," Jessica explained. "I decided I was going to find the gold. I kind of got carried away. I found this map, and I went to the beach looking for clues. I dug and dug and dug—"

"I helped," Lila cut in. "I mean, it was *such* exhausting work. The sand was sticking to us, the sun was beating down . . ."

Jessica shot Lila a glare.

"You girls must have thought you were on the right track, to work so hard," Maggie commented.

Jessica pulled her eyes away from Lila. "We were excited because *I* found these clues. They led us to the tiny bag that had your locket in it," she finished.

"But the pot of gold—that's only a myth,"

Maggie said. "So where did the map come from? And the clues?"

"I made up the map," Steven said. "It was really dumb. I just wanted to play a trick on Jessica. But then our sister, Elizabeth, found out what I was doing and decided to play a trick on both of us. Because I'd just played this practical joke on her and Jessica wouldn't share the map with her. . . . Well, anyway, she planted the fake clues—never knowing they'd actually lead to the spot where your locket was buried."

"Good grief. That *is* quite a story," Maggie said. "But—how did you pick Sunset Beach in the first place?"

"Well, I—I—," Steven was staring across the room at an open window. There was a scratching noise, and then he thought he caught a glimpse of blond hair. Or was it marmalade-colored fur? He couldn't tell. Whatever it was, it was trying to get into the house. "Maggie, do you have a cat?" he asked.

"No," Maggie said. She turned in her chair, following Steven's gaze.

All of a sudden, a tree branch outside the window broke—revealing Elizabeth!

Maggie gasped in surprise. "Are—are there two of you, then?" she asked Jessica. "Or are there even more? Is another girl going to show up and scare me out of my wits?"

"No! That's my twin sister," Jessica said. "Elizabeth."

"Hmm." Maggie stood up and walked over to the window. She seemed to have lost her cheery mood all of a sudden. "Well, Elizabeth. Would you like to come in and join us? Or do you prefer eavesdropping and spying on people when they're not aware of you?"

Elizabeth looked hurt. She backed away from the window, and her mouth trembled, as if she were about to start crying.

Steven winced. He didn't want Elizabeth to be *that* upset. Crying wasn't part of his plan. *Maybe she should get to meet Maggie,* he thought. *Since she's the one who's actually read her books.* It wouldn't be fair, of course—but anything to keep Elizabeth from turning into a basket case.

"Maggie, I'm sorry Elizabeth's acting kind of rudely," he said. "But it's not what you think. She's not spying or anything—she just really wants to meet you. She loves you."

"Loves me?" Maggie repeated.

"Yeah. She's a big fan," Steven said. "Right, Jessica?"

Jessica glanced at the window. Elizabeth was still standing there, looking sort of pathetic. "It's true," Jessica said, nodding. "She's been wanting to meet you for a long time. She's even writing a play based on one of your stories. She's a really good writer, so it'll probably be great—you don't have to worry about that."

Steven remembered the phony call he'd made to Elizabeth, and how eager she'd sounded to talk to

Maggie. She'd had so many questions—way too many for him. She deserved to be in there too. "Please, don't turn her away," Steven begged. "Meeting you would be a major highlight of her whole life."

"Well. Since you put it that way," Maggie said. She turned back to Elizabeth. "Come on in and have a shortbread with us."

Elizabeth's heart was pounding with excitement. She couldn't believe she was actually sitting in Maggie Sullivan's living room, chatting with one of her favorite writers of all time—or how silly she must have looked, crouching by the window like a squirrel.

"I'm sorry I didn't knock," Elizabeth apologized. "I wasn't trying to be rude. But Steven and Jessica are so mad at me—"

"Not to mention Lila," Lila added with a pointed look.

"Right. Lila too," Elizabeth said. "They didn't want me to come today. I followed them on my bike."

"Quite a bit of intrigue for a Saturday morning," Maggie commented. "Usually I just read the newspaper and have a pot of strong tea."

Elizabeth smiled. Strong tea—just like the book said! "Well, I really am sorry about intruding. I know you don't like that. I just couldn't help myself."

"Urges that can't be resisted are the stuff of great stories," Maggie said. "I understand you're a writer yourself."

"I write a little bit," Elizabeth admitted. "Nothing like you."

"Don't be so sure," Maggie said. "Your sister tells me you're writing a play. Which story is it based on?"

"'Fool's Paradise,'" Elizabeth said. "Only I'm kind of stuck."

"Well, maybe I could help you. Not now—we'd bore the others here to death. But another time, Elizabeth," Maggie said.

Elizabeth nearly leaped with joy. "I'd love that! Thank you."

"'Tis nothing, considering what you all have done for me." Maggie gazed longingly at the locket in her palm. "You know, this locket means so much to me. It was a gift from my husband, Patrick, on our wedding day back in Ireland. Shortly after Patrick passed away, I was down at Sunset Beach, swimming, trying to get on with my life. I took the locket off and put it in that tiny purple bag. But when I came out of the water, it was gone. I thought it had been stolen!" Maggie said. "I felt just awful. It was one of the few presents Patrick had ever given me, and to lose it after losing him . . . it was terrible."

"That's so sad," Jessica said, wiping a tear off her cheek.

"Wow," Steven said. "No wonder you were so surprised to see it again."

"Surprised! Good grief, you nearly gave me a heart attack!" Maggie laughed.

"I'm sorry," Elizabeth said. "We didn't mean to shock you. And I knew you didn't like having to talk to us—"

"Whoever said that, love?" Maggie asked.

"Well . . . I kept trying to get in touch with you, but your phone number was unlisted, and no one had an address for you, and the lady at the writers' association said you'd dropped out of touch—"

"That wouldn't be Gwen Bramblyhedge, would it?" Maggie asked, a twinkle in her eye.

"Gwen who?" Lila said.

"Well, yes, it was," Elizabeth said. "Why? Do you know her?"

"Know her? Elizabeth, she's the reason I quit going to those meetings," Maggie said with a laugh. "She's the most overbearing, self-indulgent, stupid person I ever met! How she ever got to be vice president of a writers' group is beyond me. The woman can't even spell her own name."

"Well, you have to admit, Bramblyhedge does sound kind of tough to spell," Jessica said.

Steven laughed. "Is that *hedge* with two *g*'s or one?"

Maggie laughed. "I'd like to push her into a brambly hedge! She was always setting me up to talk here, and lecture there, and give this and that newspaper an interview, and sign my books at such and such a bookstore—just to make herself look good," Maggie explained. "I suppose she thought she was helping me. But I had no interest in that. I only care about my writing."

Elizabeth nodded. "So that's when you decided to sort of drop out of the public eye?"

"Yes," Maggie said. "I prefer to be on my own. That way I can focus on my writing, instead of having everyone else focus on me. Because after all, I'm not that interesting."

"I don't know about that," Steven said. "I saw all those pictures in the hallway—you know, the black-and-white ones, with those movie stars?"

"That's when I came to California. I thought I was going to write stories for Hollywood," Maggie said.

Elizabeth nodded. She remembered reading about that in one of her books.

"You're kidding!" Jessica exclaimed. "Hollywood?"

Maggie rolled her eyes. "Believe me, it's not as glamorous as it sounds. First they turned a few of my books into movies. That was fine. But then they changed the entire story of my favorite book ever—"

"*Nothing to Lose*?" Elizabeth guessed, on the edge of her seat.

"Exactly. Only it turned out I had quite a bit to lose!" Maggie shook her head. "It was an awful picture, and I gave up working in movies. That's when I moved to Sweet Valley and started a more secluded life. Well." She stood up. "I'm afraid I've been talking your ears off all this time! You must be frightfully bored."

"I'm not bored at all," Lila said, gazing at Maggie with what looked like newfound respect. "I want to hear more about this Hollywood stuff. Who starred in the movies? Did you ever date anyone famous? Did you live in Beverly Hills? Did you go to the Academy Awards—"

"I want to know more about your life in Ireland," Steven said, grabbing another piece of shortbread. "Did you grow up in county Cork?"

"What was that like?" Jessica asked. "I really want to go to Ireland. And London too. And the Riviera. And—"

"But we don't want to take up *too* much of your time," Elizabeth said. "You might want to get back to writing."

"You're a very polite bunch," Maggie said. "And you've ridden your bikes all this way just to see me and bring me my locket. I couldn't be happier. And if you just wait here a second, I have something I'd like to give each of you. I'll be right back."

Elizabeth sucked in her breath, watching Maggie head upstairs. What was she going to give them?

Thirteen

"She doesn't have to give us anything," Jessica said as soon as Maggie had left the room. "I mean, really. She could give me an old pencil of hers and I'd be happy. It could be broken in half and have teeth marks on it, for all I care."

"She's pretty cool, isn't she?" Steven mused.

"Yeah," Lila said with a sigh.

"She's even nicer than I imagined," Elizabeth added.

They all sat in silence for a minute or two.

Jessica hadn't expected to enjoy meeting Maggie so much. She had almost forgotten her excitement over the prospect of finding gold. Somehow that just didn't seem so important anymore.

Am I crazy? she wondered. *Or am I actually starting to feel sort of bad about getting so wrapped up in finding a pot of gold?*

She turned to her brother and said something she never would have imagined herself saying. "Look, I'm sorry," she said. "I was way out of line with that pot of gold thing. I shouldn't have stolen your map, Steven."

"You wouldn't have stolen it if I hadn't drawn it in the first place," Steven said. "I guess that was kind of unfair."

"Yeah, that was pretty rotten," Jessica agreed. As noble as she felt apologizing, she was pleased that Steven took some of the blame too. She turned to Elizabeth. "But then I yelled at you and said you couldn't have any of my gold. Like it was even my gold to begin with. Sorry."

"It's OK," Elizabeth said. "Except for the part about me buying ugly clothes with the money." She looked at Lila, raising an eyebrow.

"Sorry," Lila muttered.

"Yeah, well, at least you didn't call Elizabeth and pretend to be Maggie," Steven said. "Like I did. Sorry, Elizabeth, that was out of hand."

"Maybe if I had, she wouldn't have caught me!" Jessica giggled. "I am a woman, after all."

"Woman?" Steven scoffed.

"You wouldn't have fooled me for long either," Elizabeth said with a smile. "But I shouldn't have tried to get you both back by burying those phony clues. I'm really sorry."

"I guess we all got carried away with this luck thing," Jessica said. "I'm never watching a lottery drawing again."

They were all quiet again for a moment or two. Then Jessica turned to her best friend. "Lila? Do you have anything to say?"

"Do you think she has any more iced tea?" Lila asked, trying to peer into the kitchen.

"About the buried treasure, I mean." Jessica said, exasperated.

Before Lila could answer, Maggie came back down the stairs. She walked up to Elizabeth and placed a small gold coin in her hand. "One for you . . . one for you . . ." She handed one to Jessica, and then Lila, and finally Steven.

"Whoa!" Jessica cried. "What's *this?*"

"These are gold coins I brought with me from Ireland. They're very old," Maggie explained with a smile. "The legend says that as long as you hold on to the gold coins, your lives will be filled with luck and good fortune."

"But—it looks like you're giving them all to us," Steven said. "Shouldn't you keep one?"

"I've got one left now," Maggie said. "But one is all I need."

Elizabeth rubbed the coin in her hand. Maggie Sullivan had actually given her a real gold coin! Something that had belonged to her!

"Lila, check this out," Jessica said excitedly. "Do you think I could put it on a necklace?"

"No way. I had the idea first," Lila said. "We can't have matching necklaces. That's, like, *so* fifth grade."

Maggie smiled at Elizabeth. "Come by tomorrow afternoon at three, and we'll work on your play."

Elizabeth's eyes widened. "Really? You mean it?"

"Of course I mean it," Maggie said. "What do you take me for, a liar?"

"No," Elizabeth said with a laugh. "You know what? This gold coin is already working. Because my biggest wish just came true."

"Easy, isn't it?" Maggie said. "Just don't ever lose it."

"Oh, I won't," Elizabeth said. "You can count on that."

"Hi, Jessica. It's Rick. I was wondering. Do you want to go to the movies tonight? Uh—with me, I mean?"

Jessica stared at the gold coin sitting on her desk. Man, that thing worked fast!

Not that she needed any help where Rick was concerned, but still. "That sounds great, Rick," she told him. "What time?"

"I don't know. We could get a pizza first and then see the seven o'clock show," Rick suggested. "My brother already said he'd pick us up afterward."

"Cool!" Jessica said. "I'll ask my mom and dad if I can go and I'll call you back. But plan on it, OK?"

"OK. Bye!" Rick said.

Jessica had just hung up the phone when it rang again. She grabbed the receiver. "Rick, I said I'd call *you* back!" she said with a laugh.

"*Rick?* This is Lila. Have you lost your mind?" Lila replied.

"Oh, hi, Lila." Jessica felt a little embarrassed, but she was too excited to waste time blushing. "Rick just called me two seconds ago. We're going to a movie tonight! Isn't that awesome?"

"Cool," Lila said. "But that's nothing compared with my great news. My dad and I just patched up our argument—you know, about the leather jacket?"

"What did he say?" Jessica asked. She was in too good a mood to be bothered by Lila's competitiveness. "Is he willing to put in half the money if you do some baby-sitting? Or will he take it out of your allowance gradually, or—"

"Please," Lila interrupted. "It's much better than that. He's arranged to let me have my very own gold credit card! Isn't that incredible? Maggie was right! That gold coin really does work wonders."

Jessica fiddled with the coin on her desk. "Maybe the way the coin worked was that it made you and your dad stop arguing. Maybe that's the real good fortune. Because you know," she said, thinking of Rick, "love's way more important than money."

"Uh-huh. And I'm sure you'll be saying that the next time I offer to put some clothes on my credit card for you," Lila said.

Clothes, Jessica thought. That was exactly what she didn't have! Nothing new and exciting anyway.

And that was really all that counted, when you were going on a date with Rick Hunter.

"You know, Lila. Funny you should mention that," Jessica said. "It just dawned on me that I don't have anything to wear to the movies tonight. . . ."

"Hey, Elizabeth," Steven said, walking into the living room late Saturday afternoon. "Guess what? I just bench-pressed more weight than I ever have before. And when I went on my usual five-mile jog this afternoon, I finished a whole four minutes faster than usual. Isn't that awesome?"

"That's great," Elizabeth told him. "I'm happy for you. I mean, I'd hate to see you wearing yourself out with no results," she teased.

"It's partly my hard work. But I'm sure part of it is due to the gold coin," Steven said.

Elizabeth took her gold coin out of her pocket and tossed it into the air. "There must be something to that legend after all. Because I haven't had a luckier day in a long time. I got to meet Maggie, she promised to help with my play, you guys don't hate me anymore. . . ."

Jessica came flying down the stairs into the living room. "Guess what? I have a date with Rick tonight!" she announced. "All thanks to Maggie's gold coin!"

"I hope these things don't wear out," Steven said, prying the gold coin out of his running sneaker.

"Me too," Jessica said. "Lila's been lucky too. She just got her very own gold credit card, if you can believe that."

"I don't know if that's what Maggie was talking about when she said we'd have good fortune," Elizabeth commented. "I think she was talking about being rich in other ways. Like in spirit, and having a good life and all that."

"Sure. But having a gold credit card wouldn't hurt," Jessica said. "Hey, do you think Mom and Dad would ever consider—"

"Don't even think about it," Steven said.

"Yeah. Now you're *really* pushing your luck," Elizabeth said, and they all started laughing.

Elizabeth didn't feel as though she needed to push her luck. After meeting Maggie Sullivan, she was sure she had enough luck to last her a lifetime!

"So, did you finish your play yet?" Jessica asked Monday morning at breakfast.

"Almost," Elizabeth replied, pouring some Corny O's into her bowl.

"Well, I was thinking. . . . How about giving me a role in it? I think I'd be perfect in Maggie Sullivan's story—since I met her and all," Jessica said. "I could play that girl—what's her name?"

"Siobhan," Elizabeth replied. "But you didn't even want to read the part when I asked you to help me!"

"I was busy then," Jessica said. "I'm not now.

Come on, Elizabeth. We can put on the play at school and—"

"Actually, I think I'd make a better Siobhan than you," Elizabeth told her.

Jessica shook her head. "Are you kidding? First of all, you're the author. You can't be *in* it," Jessica argued. "Besides, I'd be more dramatic. I'm going to be on TV someday, and then you won't be able to afford me, so you'd better take advantage now."

Elizabeth grinned. "Well, thanks. I'll keep that in mind." She could just imagine Jessica playing Siobhan with some horrible-sounding, overdone Irish accent. She might as well ask *Steven*.

"I'd hurry up and hire me," Jessica warned. "You never know. I might make it on TV sooner than you think."

Will Jessica become a television celebrity? Read Sweet Valley Twins #106, **BREAKFAST OF ENEMIES,** *and find out.*

Bantam Books in the SWEET VALLEY TWINS series.
Ask your bookseller for the books you have missed.

SIGN UP FOR THE SWEET VALLEY HIGH® FAN CLUB!

Hey, girls! Get all the gossip on Sweet Valley High's® most popular teenagers when you join our fantastic Fan Club! As a member, you'll get all of this really cool stuff:

- Membership Card with your own personal Fan Club ID number
- A Sweet Valley High® Secret Treasure Box
- Sweet Valley High® Stationery
- Official Fan Club Pencil (for secret note writing!)
- Three Bookmarks
- A "Members Only" Door Hanger
- Two Skeins of J. & P. Coats® Embroidery Floss with flower barrette instruction leaflet
- Two editions of *The Oracle* newsletter
- Plus exclusive Sweet Valley High® product offers, special savings, contests, and much more!

Be the first to find out what Jessica & Elizabeth Wakefield are up to by joining the Sweet Valley High® Fan Club for the one-year membership fee of only $6.25 each for U.S. residents, $8.25 for Canadian residents (U.S. currency). Includes shipping & handling.

Send a check or money order (do not send cash) made payable to "Sweet Valley High® Fan Club" along with this form to:

SWEET VALLEY HIGH® FAN CLUB, BOX 3919-B, SCHAUMBURG, IL 60168-3919

NAME_____
(Please print clearly)

ADDRESS_____

CITY_____ STATE _____ ZIP_____
(Required)

AGE_____ BIRTHDAY_____ /_____ /_____

Offer good while supplies last. Allow 6-8 weeks after check clearance for delivery. Addresses without ZIP codes cannot be honored. Offer good in USA & Canada only. Void where prohibited by law.
©1993 by Francine Pascal   LCI-1383-123